# CHAOS RISING

**AUTHOR:**
James Collura

**EDITOR:**
Jeff Harkness

**ART DIRECTOR:**
Casey Christofferson

**LAYOUT:**
Suzy Moseby

**SWORDS & WIZARDRY CONVERSION:**
Jeff Harkness

**INTERIOR ART:**
Santa Norvaisaite, Adrian Landeros, Brett Barkley

**FRONT COVER ART:**
Michael Syrigos

**CARTOGRAPHY:**
Robert Altbauer

**COVER DESIGN:**
Casey Christofferson

**PLAYTESTERS:**
Brain Mursch, Alex Yang, Courtney Brownlee, Adam Freeman, Adam Moran, Lionel Thompson, Scott Turnbull, Jorge Santiago, and Serge Clermont.

**SPECIAL THANKS:**
To Brenda, the love of my life, for encouraging me to write this module; to Brian & Alex for all of their support; to Clark & Bill for the opportunity to be part of a great team; to Casey & Lance for all of their assistance; and to my parents for fostering my love for reading and for buying me a red box, a white crayon, six blue dice, and a book that unlocked my imagination.

**NECROMANCER Games™**

**NECROMANCER Games**
ISBN: 978-1-62283-941-4
SW PoD

# Table of Contents

# CHAOS RISING

By James Collura

An adventure for 4 to 6 characters of 10th to 12th level and above.

# INTRODUCTION

A challenging adventure for four to six characters of 10th to 12th level (and above), *Chaos Rising* offers an excellent add-on to any fantasy campaign. The location of the Devil's Finger — the main site of the adventure — can be placed in any mountain chain. The benefactor the characters serve is generic and customizable for your campaign; where the party meets the benefactor is similarly up to your discretion. The deities presented in the adventure — Dwurfater, Orcus, and the Faceless Lord — may also be changed to fit your campaign. The major enemy, Lord Raob, could easily be a reoccurring enemy in the campaign. The timing of the adventure is a fortnight before a blood moon. Since blood moons are rare and not easily predictable, this event could be added to your campaign at any time.

The adventure begins when a benefactor implores the characters to take on a nearly impossible quest to retrieve a demon's amulet. First, the heroes must scale a 750-foot-tall monument to reach an ancient dwarven castle known in modern times as the Citadel. Arriving at the Citadel, the characters evade the machinations of an evil lord and travel through time to acquire a key that unlocks an ancient vault created by a long-forgotten demon prince. In the Citadel, the heroes confront both demons and undead. Once the key is obtained, the characters wait for the appointed hour: the rising of a blood moon. Once the vault is bathed in the rising moon's crimson glow, the adventure concludes as the characters enter the vault, awaken and confront the avatar of a demon prince, and recover pieces of a riddle that allows them to seize the prince's amulet.

## THE LEGEND OF THE FACELESS LORD

In the beginning, when the fires of creation cooled and the first mortals began to walk the Material Plane, the greater gods gathered to divide the multiverse. Those of weal took the most pleasant planes. They shared these planes with their allies and made them as they saw fit. Thus, the heavens were created. As well, some of the evil spawned by creation banded together and formed a great army that seized the remaining planes. Thus, the hells were created. These lords of hell demanded tribute from all of evil bent. Along with this tribute, they demanded subservience to their will and rule.

Not all were happy with this division between good and evil. Some were left with only the most inhospitable and deformed areas of the multiverse. These beings challenged this so-called natural order of the celestials and the devils. They cried out in dissention and formed a great horde that ravaged the planes. These were the first demons. Sent forth to lead an army of celestials against the demons was a being of absolute rigidity and perfection. His body was fair and his mind keen. This beacon of light had no visage but a perfectly smooth face from which blinding light emitted. He was known as the Faceless Lord.

Unfortunately, the Faceless Lord was led astray during the battles with the demons. He learned to revel in his brilliance on the battlefield, and so his vanity was his undoing. He began to see the demons not as the vile beacons of lawlessness, but as oppressed beings subjugated by both celestials and devils. Soon, he was swayed to the side of disorder and led many of his celestial followers to the dark. Who tempted this icon of perfection? Orcus? Demogorgon? Who can say?

What is known is that when the combined armies of the good-aligned planes overtook the demonic hordes, they cast the demons into the Abyss, the worst of all planes. To mark his sin permanently, the greater gods of good stripped the Faceless Lord of his perfection. He became a liquefied and ever-changing deity. Some say that a certain greater power remarked that this was done so all would know the Faceless Lord for what he was: ever-changing and devoid of trust. The Faceless Lord is the personification of chaos. He is always changing, always plotting, and always thoroughly evil. He is known by some as Jubilex.

# ADVENTURE BACKGROUND

The adventure begins at the Devil's Finger, a 750-foot-tall granite monument. At the apex of this monolith is an ancient and abandoned dwarven castle. Although the true name of the castle is Dwurschmiede, this name is lost to the ages, and the castle is known in modern times simply as the Citadel. The Citadel surrounds a gigantic cube of obsidian. Impervious to magic, the true nature of the Obsidian Vault is known to only a few scholars.

The Obsidian Vault is a creation of Jubilex, the Faceless Lord. Like most powerful demons, the Faceless Lord spent considerable effort in hiding his soul, which was made manifest in the form of an amulet. To protect his amulet, the Faceless Lord created the Obsidian Vault. Crafted from the then-dwindling fires of creation, the Obsidian Vault is impervious to everything, whether magical or mundane, mortal or divine. After placing his soul within the vault, the Faceless Lord let loose the great cube and sent it wandering through the planes.

For reasons unknown, several thousand years ago, the vault appeared on the characters' home plane and crashed on top of a mountain. As a result of the magical energies that protect the vault, combined with the force of the impact, the Devil's Finger was formed. Ancient dwarves discovered and revered the monolith as a work of wonder. Soon, some wicked dwarves began to revere the Faceless Lord on the grounds that, out of chaos, he constructed the vault, an example of nearly perfect craftsmanship. Since the dwarven pantheon abhors chaos, the leader of the dwarven gods, Dwurfater, grew wrathful.

The vault's protections were beyond even the power of Dwurfater to breach. Using all of his strength, Dwurfater could not penetrate the vault. Only through placating the inherent evilness of the vault by sacrificing dwarven lives did Dwurfater gather the strength to bore an opening through the stone and create a door. As tears ran down Dwurfater's face, many dwarves gave their lives to aid their god in his task. Blood washed the entire Devil's Finger as generations of dwarves were sacrificed for this gruesome but necessary deed.

Though the penetration was finally accomplished, Dwurfater was too weakened to open the door he created and seize control of the amulet, so with his last bit of strength he crafted a key such that mortals could accomplish what he could not. The Faceless Lord learned of what Dwurfater planned and attempted to stop the followers from securing the amulet that contained his soul. Arriving at the Citadel, the Faceless Lord's avatar rushed after Dwurfater's disciples and entered the vault.

In the battle that ensued between the Faceless Lord and Dwurfater's followers, the dwarves accomplished their true task: As the Faceless Lord entered the vault, Dwurfater's strength returned, and he closed the door. The Faceless Lord was trapped inside with his amulet.

After this great victory by the dwarves, they built Dwurschmiede, the Citadel, a structure designed to safeguard the vault. The Citadel was to bar those who would seek to free the Faceless Lord or take his amulet for themselves. Also, the Citadel was created to guard the key used by Dwurfater to lock the vault. To remember the bloody sacrifice of the dwarves and to placate the evil that imprisons the Faceless Lord, the door to the vault appears only once every 400 years when a blood moon rises and bathes the Devil's Finger in an unnatural red light.

Dwurfater assisted in the creation of the Citadel. He infused his divinity into the Citadel to protect the only means of returning the Faceless Lord to the world: the key. One protection prevents anyone from directly accessing any other plane (such as the Astral Plane for teleportation) while on the Devil's Finger. This divine infusion also prevents anyone from contacting an evil-aligned plane for divination, summoning, or other purposes.

The second protection is stronger and unusually arcane for the dwarves. To the outside world, the Citadel appears as a great fortress with towers and walls encircling the vault. This appearance is merely a ruse, however. Through Dwurfater's guidance and divinity, these outer walls and defenses are a façade protecting the Citadel's true nature: its interior is actually a demiplane.

The interior of the Citadel exists and ages the same as the outer world. Entrance to the Citadel, however, is limited to a single planar gate inside a great barbican. This planar gate is far from simple, for it uses temporal wells to send intruders through time. Only with a *portal rune* (described in **Chapter One**) can someone gain access to the actual Citadel.

Within this interior demiplane, an entire clan of dwarves — Clan Flammeaxte — willingly submitted to living apart as protectors of the Citadel. Their mission was simple: prevent anyone from acquiring the key.

To further guard the key, Dwurfater fashioned a second demiplane. Like the first planar gate, the second gate uses time itself as a defense. Only with a special rune known only to the lord or king of the Citadel may one enter this second plane. In the second plane, the dwarves created many wards and guardians to protect the key. Disguising the second demiplane as catacombs to baffle aggressors, the dwarves have thus far succeeded in their task. No one has acquired the key.

During the millennia since the first dwarves stood guard in the Citadel, many armies have marched on the Devil's Finger seeking the key as a first step to acquiring the demon's amulet. Even with the temporal portals, the clan of dwarves, and the confusion created by shifts in time and space, evil was undeterred from acquiring the Faceless Lord's amulet-soul.

Two such undeterred armies were those of the demon prince Orcus and, later, a legion of undead commanded by a powerful priest named Giltz. Orcus, a deceiver, learned of the Citadel's nature. Knowing that Dwurfater's protections prevented direct entry, Orcus turned a goodly priest to evil and taught him a way to overcome the protection and open a *gate* to Orcus' home plane. Eventually, possibly with the characters' help, the dwarves pushed back the demons and closed the unusual gate.

Later, Giltz accomplished what Orcus could not: He and a host of undead overcame and wiped out the dwarves. Yet before Giltz could claim his prize, the last dwarves assassinated him. In his anguish, Giltz's spirit remained and now haunts the Citadel's demiplane.

Currently, the Citadel abides in a parallel plane but is abandoned and its purpose lost to the minds of human and dwarf alike. So, too, is the name of the Faceless Lord forgotten. Knowledge of him is only a whisper among those who study the arcane. To this day, the Faceless Lord stirs trapped within the vault, nursing a hatred of all dwarves. For the ironic secret of the vault, the Faceless Lord created is this: though the vault is a reliquary for the Faceless Lord's amulet, it also serves as his prison.

This situation is about to change, however. The evil Lord Raob Blackenheart has gathered an army and encamped it at the summit of the Devil's Finger. Here, he and his men are excavating the Citadel and attempting to dig down to the key's resting place. This strategy is folly, for Raob has yet to suspect that the now-ruined towers and walls are merely a ruse. It is only a matter of time before this evil lord learns of the Citadel's true nature and acquires the key.

A blood moon approaches in two weeks' time.

Enter the characters. Through the hook of your choosing, they are charged with a daunting task: acquire the key, spoil an evil lord's machinations, open the vault, and save the world — all in a day's work for heroes.

# ADVENTURE HOOKS

The adventure begins when the characters learn portions of the background from a benefactor such as a church (good or evil) or a guild (magic-user or thief), as fits your campaign and particular characters. Whichever organization or individual ultimately employs the characters, that entity is referred to hereafter as the benefactor. The benefactor's primary motivation is to obtain a demon price's amulet. What the benefactor wishes to do with the amulet depends on several issues. For example, a goodly church would wish to destroy the device, while a wizards' guild would want to study it, and an evil sect would want to use its powers to further their own fell agenda.

Here are several suggested hooks:

One of the characters owes a great debt to the benefactor, and the benefactor is now asking that the debt be paid. In a good-aligned campaign, now is the time to pay up for all that free healing at the local church. In an evil-aligned campaign, the benefactor could attempt to assassinate one of the characters and blame Raob. During that time, the benefactor approaches the characters with the helpful information as to who is trying to kill them. The benefactor lets them know of Raob.

An agent of the Faceless Lord could hire the characters. The characters have no idea that their benefactor works for the fallen celestial. Still, the characters rush off to save the day not knowing that their actions loose the Faceless Lord on the world. This is a difficult scenario because of the horrific twist that will likely take place assuming the characters overcome the Faceless Lord, just to learn seconds after their victory that they were the pawns of chaos.

If you do not want to use a benefactor, you could have the party's wizard learn of the Citadel while deep into studying a recently acquired tome (conveniently placed in the prior adventure). In the margins of the tome are notes by Sleeara, the necromancer serving Raob. The party's wizard puts together what Sleeara is planning, the location of the Citadel, and the time remaining to stop her.

Basically, ***Chaos Rising*** can take place at any time and in virtually any locale. You should be creative in starting the adventure and impress upon the characters the grave danger that threatens the realm if Raob takes the amulet for himself.

The characters and the benefactor should know a few key facts (or acquire such information from the tome, if using that hook), including the existence of the Citadel, the existence of the key, and that a demon prince's amulet lies within the vault. The benefactor should also know that Lord Raob is attempting to seize the amulet for himself. Furthermore, through an astrologer, the benefactor knows that a blood moon approaches in 14 days.

Finally, the benefactor has discovered that there is a portal into the Citadel. The benefactor might believe, as Raob does, that the Citadel is in ruins and therefore, the passageways and tunnels that lead to the key are collapsed and full of rubble. Therefore, to beat Raob to the key, the characters must use the portal, travel back through time to where the passageways are intact, and snatch the key out from under Raob.

To activate the portal, the benefactor has employed an ancient dwarven priestess. This priestess actually knows the Citadel's planar secret, but does not disclose this information under any circumstances. Instead, she marks or tattoos the necessary *portal rune* on all the characters' necks to allow them access in an effort to destroy the Faceless Lord once and for all.

The important fact that is omitted in any setup for this adventure (although wily characters might correctly guess this fact) is that the Faceless Lord is trapped within the vault. Thus, the characters should be unaware of this matter at the time they embark upon their quest.

# Players' Introduction

With a minimum of alteration, the following background is usable for most any benefactor or hook you choose — good or evil, arcane, divine, or worldly. Read or paraphrase as necessary:

The heavy eyes of your benefactor peer over the tomes and scrolls on her desk to look you square in the eye. She awaits an answer.

You and your friends received the summons less than a week ago. The urgency in tone could not be mistaken — grave danger threatens the realm.

You have been asked to retrieve a fabulous artifact, the amulet of a demon prince. Like most who have studied or encountered demons before, you know that a demon's amulet contains its soul. One who possesses such an artifact can banish the demon for centuries or even command it to heed one's will. Thus, the amulet of a minor demon in the wrong hands can be a force of destruction. The amulet of a demon prince can render anyone invincible.

To accomplish this quest, you must travel to an arid mountain chain. In the midst of these mountains stands a gigantic granite monument 750 feet high that resembles the bony knuckles of a finger. It is known as the Devil's Finger. On top of the Devil's Finger lies an ancient fortress carved directly out of the granite. Legends tell that the fortress, known today simply as the Citadel, was built by ancient dwarves. The entire complex has collapsed and is in ruins.

The dwarves built the Citadel around a gigantic cube — or vault — of obsidian. The origin of the vault is unknown; however, religious scholars working for your benefactor think that it is otherworldly in nature and predates the Citadel. Thus, these scholars assume that the Citadel was built to protect the vault.

Within the vault, the amulet lies undisturbed as it has for thousands of years. Armies laid siege to the Citadel hoping to acquire the key and the amulet. Breaking their attacks against the granite, no army succeeded. Now that no one guards the key, however, the evil Lord Raob Blackenheart might succeed where others have failed.

Although few texts and histories concerning the Citadel are extant, what is known is that once every 400 years a blood moon rises and reveals an entrance to the vault. If someone stands at the entrance at this appointed hour with a special key, then he may enter the vault. No other means magical or otherwise can penetrate the cube. The key is presumed to reside in a complex of caves and catacombs beneath the Citadel.

Your benefactor had very little interest in the Citadel until a month ago, when after 1,200 years it once again became occupied. Apparently, the evil Lord Raob and his pet necromancer are determined to find the key and open the cube. They and a small army are camped around the ruins of the Citadel and are attempting to dig their way through the collapsed halls and find the key. Going by his reputation for malice and slaughter, Raob likely intends to take the amulet and begin a campaign of carnage and bloodshed.

Your benefactor has employed astrologers and learned that a blood moon approaches in a fortnight. Your party is asked to climb the Devil's Finger, enter the Citadel, and steal the key before Lord Raob succeeds.

Naturally, this task will not be easy. First, numerous magical protections are still active in the Devil's Finger. These protections make scaling the monument with extreme caution necessary. In addition, the presence of Lord Raob and his army requires you to use stealth. Once you are on top of the Devil's Finger, you must find the main entrance to the Citadel. This entrance is believed to be within a massive barbican.

Your benefactor has devised an unusual way for you to acquire the key before Lord Raob. One of the protections that the dwarves used involved magical portals that allowed guards to travel back through time to warn of invaders. Your benefactor's scholars presume that two such portals remain today. One is at the entrance to the entrance to the Citadel's top level, and the other is a hidden entrance into the catacombs where the key lies.

Thus, you will use these portals to shift to a time when the passageways are not blocked by rock and rubble. In this alternate reality or time, the Citadel is in its full splendor, and you should therefore be able to acquire the key and return to your home time. Your benefactor has convinced an ancient dwarven priestess to inscribe the necessary *portal rune* on each of you. This tattoo will be placed on your neck and under no circumstance should fall into enemy's hands. Although nothing is known of the denizens of this other time, they should prove less hostile than dealing with Lord Raob and his army.

Once the key is acquired, your task is not over. Retrieving the key and foiling the evil lord's plans is not enough. This evil must be ended once and for all so that future generations are not caught unaware. You must enter the cube on the night of the blood moon, retrieve this amulet, and return it so that it may be destroyed, ending the vileness of the demon prince's essence.

Your benefactor's stare breaks for a moment. She licks her cracked lips and speaks harshly, "What say thee?"

# Running the Adventure

The characters start by meeting with their benefactor. After this meeting, the characters have an opportunity to prepare for the assault on the Devil's Finger, purchase supplies and items, and plan for the adventure. The benefactor also provides the characters with a device or key to activate the portals.

As explained in the Adventure Background, the characters have a fortnight to scale the Devil's Finger and retrieve an item known simply as they key. The key allows the characters to enter the vault (during a blood moon) and attempt to take the demon's amulet. The challenge is presented in five stages.

## Stage One — Assaulting the Devil's Finger (The Present)

Described in **Chapter One**, the characters must find their way into the Citadel. The Devil's Finger stands more than 750 feet tall. The challenge lies in arriving at the top of the monument without alerting Lord Raob. One obvious option is to climb the cliff face; however, not only are guards patrolling the perimeter, but several gargoyles act as natural guardians. The characters will more likely use magical means to arrive atop the great pillar. Some magical energies, such as teleportation, are suppressed by enchantments still active in the Citadel. So, arriving on top of the Devil's Finger without Raob noticing will not be easy for the characters. In addition, using magic might prove more dangerous than climbing because of a series of magical alarms that alert the small army commanded by Lord Raob and Sleeara. A third option is to use the makeshift elevator that Lord Raob uses. This approach should also prove difficult, owing to the army guards that protect the elevator. Although these guards might be easily overcome, they could sound an alarm that brings an entire army down on the characters. Once on top of the Devil's Finger, the characters penetrate the barbican near where Raob's archaeological operation is underway. After arriving, the party passes through the portal, which is activated by their personal *portal rune*, in an effort presumably to bypass hundreds of feet of rock and rubble.

## Stage Two — Entering the Portal and the Siege of Orcus (3,000 Years in the Past)

As described in **Chapter Three**, the second stage of the adventure begins once the party passes through the portal, which allows the party to enter the Citadel's demiplane. Whether the characters perceive of the change in planes is ultimately up to you. The interior of the Citadel has two portals that allow such travel through time or space. The first portal is the entrance to the Citadel's Upper Halls, the second is an archway in the Lower Halls that leads to the catacombs where the key lies.

The upper archway sends the characters to "The Siege of Orcus," an alternate plane that is similar in every way to the characters' home plane, save that the Siege of Orcus occurs almost 3,000 years in the past. Remember that the Citadel's demiplane and the characters' home plane move through time — or, age — at the same rate, but due to the planar gate's temporal nature, the characters have gone back through time. The Citadel is simply inaccessible except through the barbican portal.

During the "Siege of Orcus," the characters appear at the start of a siege by the forces of the demon prince Orcus, who desires the Faceless Lord's amulet for himself. Specifically, the characters appear shortly before Orcus bypasses the magical wards of the Citadel and opens a *gate*. Using this *gate*, a group of demons attempts to seize the dwarven king who holds the rune to access the catacombs. The characters may or may not assist the dwarves in defending the Citadel, although success might be impossible without assisting them. The characters' prime goal is to find the lower portal that will send them to the catacombs demiplane where the key lies.

## Stage Three — Acquiring the Key (The Present)

Leaving the "siege of Orcus" behind, the characters enter the catacombs as explained in **Chapter Four**. Again, the characters change planes and travel through time — to the present. Like the Citadel, this demiplane moves through time at the same rate as the party's home plane; however, the portal's temporal nature sends the characters to another era.

The catacombs were built for the dwarven kings who served the Citadel. The use of the crypts is to hide the real purpose of the area: to protect and guard the key. At the very bottom of this area is the complex with the key. The acquisition of the key is the characters' primary goal.

## Stage Four — The Return Journey and Necromantic Dreams (1,200 Years in the Past)

In **Chapter Six**, after acquiring the key, the characters return through the lower archway and travel back to the Citadel's demiplane. The characters do not, though, return to the time of the Siege of Orcus. Instead, they are sent to "Necromantic Dreams," where an army of undead decimated the dwarves. These events take place on the Citadel's demiplane 1,200 years in the past from the time of the characters' home plane. Approximately 100 years before the characters' arrival, the powerful priest led an army in an effort to take the amulet. The priest died during the final assault, so the undead have settled in the Citadel.

The "Siege of Orcus" is described in **Chapter Three**, and "Necromantic Dreams" is described in **Chapter Five**. The different rooms and physical features of the Citadel itself are detailed in **Chapter Two**, which also details various NPC parties that are seeking the key. In other words, the characters will traverse the same dungeon at least twice, but with different sets of encounters for each sojourn.

## Stage Five — Confronting the Faceless Lord (The Present)

Once the characters leave the Citadel and return to their home plane and time with the key, they may have to deal with Lord Raob and wait for the blood moon that appears at the end of the fortnight. Raob and Sleeara are possibly one of the groups of time-traveling NPCs that the characters confront during the "Siege of Orcus" or "Necromantic Dreams." During the interim between acquiring the key and the blood moon's rising, the characters may vanquish Lord Raob or perhaps join forces with him, if they are so inclined. Raob may also quite possibly discover that the Citadel was a façade and out of frustration decide to take his army elsewhere. In any event, once the blood moon rises, the characters should use the key and enter the vault of the demon prince. These events are explained in **Chapter Six**.

Within the strange obsidian cube, the characters find themselves at the threshold of a sea of ooze. In the middle of this sea is a small island with an odd cube and obelisk. In the final stage, the characters are to find pieces to a riddle to retrieve the amulet. The Faceless Lord, compelled to protect the amulet by the divine force of Dwurfater, has over the many millennia of his captivity created alternate realities and sub-planes linked together within his prison. He has hidden four stanzas of a riddle within these sub-planes. The four stanzas are necessary to open the amulet's resting place. You are encouraged to create these sub-planes, as they are a mechanism to expand the module significantly. Alternatively, you might forego the sub-planes and reach the ultimate conclusion — a direct confrontation with an avatar of the Faceless Lord. With or without the sub-planes, the adventure concludes at this point. The characters may leave the vault victorious with the demon's amulet, or they may become the latest liquefied victims of the Prince of Chaos.

## Planar Travel

In *Chaos Rising*, the characters repeatedly enter and exit planes and travel through time. You can deal with this element in two ways. The first is to explain the travel as dimensional or planar travel, as is described in the module. In other words, the heroes travel from one plane of existence to an almost identical, but finite plane of existence that happens to exist in the past. This explanation avoids many of the consistency issues with time travel.

An alternate way of dealing with this matter is to explain the travel as true temporal relocation and time travel and ignore the demiplanes. In other words, the characters are actually traveling through time, and the interior of the Citadel and catacombs exist on the characters' home plane. This explanation may prove difficult, as many consistency issues arise. There is also the inevitable, "What happens if I kill my great-great-grandfather?" A good response is, "The inertia of time and destiny flattens the smallest ripples in time." Though this statement is rather meaningless, it is sufficiently ambiguous to quiet over-anxious questioners. The time stream does not abide a paradox.

A third option is not to explain the travel at all. The mystery of the situation allows the characters to come up with their own understanding of what is occurring. With any of these options, you should be able to tailor the concept to what your players will most enjoy.

## Chronology of Events

| | |
|---|---|
| **Eons ago** | The creation of the universe. The crafting of the vault by the Faceless Lord. |
| **10,000 years ago** | The vault crashes down on the characters' world and forms the Devil's Finger. Dwarves begin to revere it. |
| **9,000 years ago** | Dwurfater tricks the Faceless Lord and imprisons him in his vault. Construction begins on Dwurschmiede, the Citadel. Dwurfater creates two demiplanes to protect the key. |
| **3,000 years ago** | Orcus lays siege to the Citadel in an attempt to acquire the Faceless Lord's amulet for himself. The events of Stage Two take place. |
| **1,300 years ago** | The priest Giltz succeeds in destroying the last dwarves occupying the Citadel. He dies in battle. |
| **1,200 years ago** | The events of Stage Four take place. |
| **1 year ago** | Lord Raob learns of the amulet and its unspeakable power. He begins his quest to acquire it. |
| **1 month ago** | Lord Raob arrives at the Devil's Finger and begins to dig down toward the key. The characters' benefactor begins to learn of what Raob is trying to accomplish. |
| **Today** | The characters learn of Raob's plan from their benefactor. In the next two weeks, the events of Stage One and, later, Stage Three take place. |
| **2 weeks from today** | A blood moon rises and shows the door into the Citadel. The events of Stage Five take place. |

# PLAYING EFFECTIVE NPCs

This module includes a number of NPCs and NPC parties. A major NPC, of course, is the Faceless Lord. Raob and Sleeara are attempting to seize the amulet in the present; Lord Galm fights the forces of Orcus in the past. As well, numerous parties of "time-traveling" NPCs (as described in **Chapter Two**) await the characters.

Playing these NPCs effectively is a challenge, especially since the NPCs are not necessarily set encounters. Having completely new groups of NPCs jumping into the picture may not suit your game. If the adventure seems too hard for the characters, these NPCs allow you to scale the difficulty. For example, one change could be substituting Lord Raob with one of your campaign's reoccurring enemies. Another change could be not using an NPC party if the characters are bogged down in one of the Citadel levels. Furthermore, you could use your own NPC party that gains access to the Citadel upon learning what the characters are trying to accomplish.

Whether you use your own NPCs or those described in this adventure, understanding their motivations as well as their powers is important for playing them effectively with the encounters and events described in this adventure.

# MAPS AND ENCOUNTER NUMBERING

Since the characters traverse the same "maps" twice in some circumstances, having a different map numbering and encounter system is necessary. Also, some of the encounters are not keyed to a specific place. Thus, the encounters are presented alphabetically with the chapter number (i.e., I-A). For the map references, the first letter indicates the specific map and the second is the Area number (i.e., A-1 refers to Map A and Area 1).

# MODIFICATIONS TO THE ADVENTURE

Modifications to this adventure are not only recommended, they are expected. This adventure is written in such a way that it can take place on any world, in any campaign. These events could occur virtually anywhere.

A benefactor and evil demon are required. The benefactor, however, need not necessarily be good. An evil party could be hired by an evil deity to fetch the amulet for themselves. The demon could be the Faceless Lord or a long-forgotten demon of your own making. Likewise, the dwarves in this module could be any race that died out long ago or some other campaign-specific race.

Additionally, as was already mentioned, the NPCs are an easy target for modification to make the adventure more or less difficult. **Chapters Three** and **Five** are designed in such a way that you can tailor entire sections of encounters. In **Chapter Six**, you are expected to expand the sub-planes to provide strange and exciting locales for your campaign that the characters might not normally encounter.

One final note: Some encounters in this adventure are written with boxed, read-aloud description text. These descriptions are provided for your benefit. Whether you use the descriptions or not is up to you. Yet their purpose is to provide you with important pieces of dialogue, complex area descriptions, and ideas. The best descriptions for your players are yours. Consider the descriptions provided as

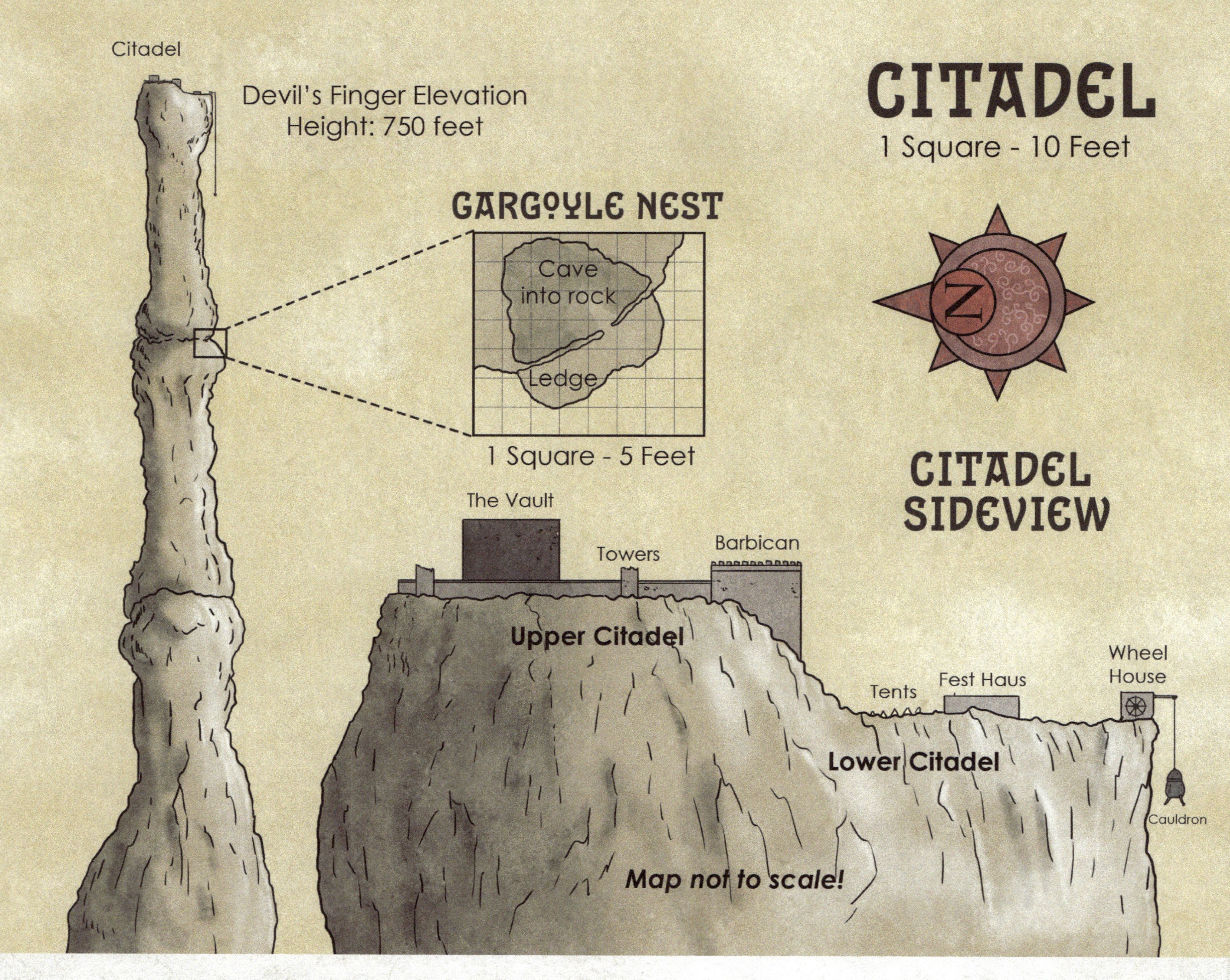

CITADEL
1 Square - 10 Feet
N
CITADEL SIDEVIEW
Devil's Finger Elevation
Height: 750 feet
GARGOYLE NEST
Cave into rock
Ledge
1 Square - 5 Feet
Citadel
The Vault
Towers
Barbican
Upper Citadel
Tents
Fest Haus
Wheel House
Cauldron
Lower Citadel
Map not to scale!

# CHAPTER ONE:
## ASSAULT ON THE DEVIL'S FINGER

helpful suggestions, not constraining requirements.

The adventure begins with the characters arriving at a valley within three miles of the Devil's Finger. How the characters arrive at this locale is up to you. Arriving at the remote location might be a difficult challenge for the characters; however, since time is of the essence (pun intended), having the benefactor described in the introduction spend the necessary funds to send the party via *teleport* to a grove of dead trees a few miles from the Devil's Finger might be easier. This adventure assumes that you have managed to get the characters to an area near the base of the Devil's Finger undetected by the agents of evil on the summit.

## THE DEVIL'S FINGER

The Devil's Finger rises above one end of the valley. On all sides of the valley, dark mountains loom. Thunderstorms are common in the afternoon, and occasional strong winds have made the valley floor nearly barren. These strong winds impose a –2 to-hit penalty to ranged attacks and hamper those who attempt to fly (flying speed reduced by 25%).

## WARNING CUBES

A *warning cube* is a six-inch silver cube with intricate runes covering its surface. The cube constantly detects a specific effect out to a 30-foot radius. Things that can be detected include animals or plants, evil, good, magic, poison, scrying, secret doors, and snares and pits. Once an effect is detected, a *magic mouth* activates on the cube and shouts a specific phrase designated by the creator.

The *warning cubes* used by Sleeara are keyed to *detect magic*. Anyone carrying magical items and passing within 30 feet of a cube activates the *magic mouth*. The *magic mouth* begins to yell "ALERT!" repeatedly. A guard has a 3-in-6 chance to hear an activated cube.

The Devil's Finger resembles the bones of a humongous, three-jointed finger. It is more than 750 feet tall and made of granite. Two flat elevations are at the top of the Finger. The lower elevation has a number of rudimentary structures that are carved directly from the stone. These structures include the Fest Haus (**Encounter I-D**) and the Wheel House (**Encounter I-E**).

The Wheel House is a recent addition commissioned by Lord Raob. He placed an enormous cauldron at the end of a very thick rope connected to an immense wheel. The cauldron is large enough to accommodate five creatures. Lord Raob uses the Wheel House as an elevator to supply and move troops. Here and the landing area (**Encounter I-F**) see almost constant activity, making them two of the most heavily-guarded areas.

The higher elevation is the Citadel itself. Like buildings on the lower elevation, the Citadel is carved out of the Finger. A large barbican allows entry from the lower elevation to the higher elevation. In addition, within the barbican is the first magic portal — through which the characters must enter (**Encounter I-G**) in order to gain access to the Citadel's interior.

Visible in the center of the Citadel is the upper two-thirds of the massive obsidian cube that houses the demon's amulet. This cube is referred to as the vault. The Citadel flows around the vault, although the walls and towers that encircle the vault are devastated. The disrepair and collapsed walls and towers have in turn toppled the Citadel's two main levels, leaving rubble blocking nearly all of the passages. The dig (**Encounter I-C**) is slowly working through solid granite in an effort to reach the key. Until a week ago, Lord Raob made little progress. Now, Sleeara is personally overseeing the operation. Due to her motivational skills, the men have dug down nearly 100 feet. They have yet to discover any artifacts or remains from the "interior." Sleeara is starting to suspect the truth of the Citadel, that it is merely a façade.

Archers from Lord Raob's army watch the valley floor. During the day, the archers have a 1-in-6 chance to notice the characters far below, even if the characters approach in the open. At night, seeing anything that is not lit is nearly impossible for the archers. If the characters use a light source, the archers have a 4-in-6 chance to notice the approaching characters.

## ASCENT

The characters cannot *teleport* to the top of the Devil's Finger. Dwurfater infused the Citadel with magical energies that cause two effects that affect the adventure. The first effect is that contact with the Astral Plane is impossible; thus, spells such as *teleport* do not function around the Citadel. Second, spells cast within 100 feet around or on the Devil's Finger that contact other planes do not function unless the contact is to a non-evil plane. Thus, summoning spells targeting evil creatures fail; *gate* and divine spells to evil planes also fail. Both magical enchantments are permanent and imbued in the stone.

Once at the base of the Devil's Finger, the characters may attempt to climb it. Each side of the Devil's Finger is smooth granite that flows in and out over the knobby protrusions or knuckles. Although natural edges can assist the characters in their ascent, the climb is still very difficult for non-thieves. Characters have a 40% chance of slipping and falling 3d6 feet for every 50 feet they climb; characters can make a saving throw to grab a protruding rock to arrest their fall or they take 1d6 points of damage per 10 feet fallen. In addition, the gargoyles (**Encounter I-A**) make this method even harder.

<table>
<tr><td colspan="2" align="center">INTRODUCTORY CHARACTERISTICS</td></tr>
</table>

**Wandering Monsters:** Patrols are infrequent beneath the Devil's Finger, as described above. This table is based on the party being at the top of the Devil's Finger. Check once every 10 minutes on 1d12:

| 1d12 | Encounter |
|------|-----------|
| 1 | Sleeara and 4 guards (from **Area I-C**) |
| 2 | Lord Raob and 4 guards (from **Area I-D**) |
| 3–5 | 1d4 guards |
| 6 | 1d4 gargoyles (from **Area I-A**) |
| 7–12 | No encounter |

**Shielding:** Spells cannot penetrate the vault (**Area A-7**). Nothing can damage or see beyond its jet-black obsidian walls. Ancient magical protections prevent anyone from traversing through the Astral Plane in and around the Citadel and the top of the Devil's Finger. Thus, astral travel and teleportation are impossible on, within, or 500 years around the Devil's Finger. In addition, summoning and similar spells that target other planes function only if the target of the spell is Lawful or Neutral.

**Detections:** Characters detect strong evil and overwhelming magic from the vault (**Area A-7**) due to the presence of the Faceless Lord and his amulet. Also, the Devil's Finger itself radiates magical energies.

**Standard Features:** Unless otherwise noted, all doors are on a central pivot and made of stone.

**Map Used:** Map A: The Devil's Finger.

Characters may attempt to *fly*, *levitate*, or use some other magical means of ascent. Sleeara (**Encounter I-C**) placed a number of *warning cubes* on the perimeter of the army's base. These *warning cubes* are spaced evenly 100 feet apart on the perimeter. In between each *warning cube* are oil-fueled torches; although wind-resistant, they frequently blow out. A torch near where the party "arrives" has a 25% chance of being out.

Characters may also attempt to use the "cauldron-elevator" built by Lord Raob. See **Encounter I-F** for more details. This means of ascent, however, is very closely watched and most likely leads to detection.

Presuming the characters find a way to ascend to the Devil's Finger (most likely by *fly* and *invisibility*), they may have several encounters during their ascent. This initial set of encounters should be suspenseful but not overly difficult for the characters (unless Lord Raob's men spot them). They should feel that they are being challenged, but not taxed to their limits — that is for later.

# Encounter I-A: Gargoyles

Native gargoyles have taken up residence two-thirds of the way up the Devil's Finger. Their nest, little more than a small ledge in the granite, is located on the east side. This lair is more a repository of shiny objects and bits of wood than an actual nest, since the gargoyles sleep hanging on the Finger's surface during the day. More active at night, the gargoyles care little if the characters arrive on top of the Finger. However, while climbing the face of the formation, the characters are fair game to the gargoyles. The creatures' primitive minds believe that a new but dangerous food source has arrived.

The gargoyles lazily circle the Finger at dusk and dawn, creating an ominous image. During the day, they sleep with their wings folded over themselves, as still and silent as stone. Sleeping gargoyles are difficult to see. A climbing character may accidentally touch one of the gargoyles during the ascent of the upper portion of the citadel. If a character attempts to climb to the Citadel, he or she has a 20% chance of touching one of the creatures.

At night, the gargoyles fly, taking the occasional guard from above as a meal. The gargoyles like to linger near the perimeter torchlight and pull prey into the darkness between torches. Sleeara feeds the gargoyles occasionally by staking a member of Raob's army who "disappoints" her into the ground near the perimeter of the Citadel. The gargoyles are used to the strong winds by the Devil's Finger and are not affected by them.

**Gargoyles (10):** HD 4; HP 32, 30x3, 29, 27, 26x2, 23, 20; AC 5[14]; Atk 2 claws (1d3), bite (1d4), horn (1d6); **Move** 9 (fly 15); **Save** 13; AL C; **CL/XP** 6/400; **Special:** +1 or better magic weapon to hit. (*Monstrosities* 185)

**Tactics:** A single gargoyle that spots or is otherwise made aware of the party's presence gathers two other gargoyles before attacking. Thereafter, all three attempt to knock the "shiniest" party member (wearing gleaming armor, has a large gem, and so forth) to the ground below. The gargoyles are cowards at heart and do their best not to engage the characters directly. If the gargoyle nest is threatened, then the entire wing attacks the characters until a bargain is made (for more shiny objects) or one group or the other is dead.

The archer guards above have a 4-in-6 chance to notice the characters if a battle ensues with the gargoyles. If spotted, the guards inform Sleeara, who engages the characters (as described in **Encounter I-C**).

**Treasure:** Stuffed into a large crack on a small three-foot ledge is the gargoyles' treasure. Numerous skulls, pieces of bone, and odd bits of metal are crammed into this crack. Far back in the space is a *+3 bastard sword* that requires five minutes of sorting and throwing items over the edge to acquire. Such actions, however, almost certainly grab the attention of the guards.

# Atop the Devil's Finger

## Encounter I-B: Guards

Lord Raob's army is 98 members strong on and around the Devil's Finger. These men are both guards and manual laborers being used to dig down to the key. The guards work in three shifts: they dig for eight hours, rest for the next eight, then assume sentry duty for the final eight hours. These shifts rotate so that a crew is always digging, resting, and guarding. There are 30 men per crew.

At any one time, 30 men are working at the dig (**Area A-3**), 30 sleeping in tents outside of the Fest Haus (**Area A-4**), and 30 on guard. Of the men on guard, 15 patrol the perimeter in teams of two or three, 12 occupy the Wheel House (**Area A-5**), and the remaining three guards assist Sleeara in her motivational efforts at the dig (**Area A-3**).

The remaining eight guards are sergeants who command the men and serve as Raob's personal guards.

**Guards, Male or Female Humans (90):** HD 4; AC 5[14]; Atk polearm (1d8+1) or longbow x2 (1d6); **Move** 12; **Save** 13; AL N; **CL/XP** 4/120; **Special:** none. (*Monstrosities* 256)
**Equipment:** black enameled chainmail, white cape, polearm, longbow, 30 arrows, 1d4 gems (1d10x10 gp)

**Sergeants, Male or Female Humans (Ftr6) (8):** HD 6; HP 47, 45, 43, 41x2, 39, 37, 34; AC 5[14]; Atk bastard sword (1d8) or longbow x2 (1d6); **Move** 12; **Save** 9; **CL/XP** 6/400; **Special:** multiple attacks (5) vs. creatures with 1 or fewer HD.
**Equipment:** black chainmail, red cape, bastard sword, longbow, 30 arrows, 1d4 gems (1d10x10 gp).

**Tactics:** If a "credible enemy" is spotted, a large bell rings out at the Fest Haus. This bell was taken from a church as plunder and put to use as a warning device. A credible enemy is one that presents a potential threat to the dig, Sleeara, or Raob. If the general alarm is sounded, the army springs into action. After 1d4+2 minutes, the guards at the dig arrive at the Fest Haus. The guards who were asleep pick up their weapons and are ready to engage after 1d6+2 minutes. After 10 minutes, the dig guards are ready for battle. The guards at the Wheel House remain in position to defend the cauldron elevator.

The guards' tactics are simple: charge and kill. The sergeants lead sorties against the enemy, striking at the largest target first. If casualties drop their numbers to 50%, the guards flee to regroup. Sleeara and Raob's tactics are listed separately in **Encounters I-C** and **I-D**.

## Encounter I-C: Sleeara and the Dig (Area A-1)

The dig is near the barbican's west tower. Digging down into the tough granite, Raob and his men are slowly inching their way toward where they presume the key lies. The men work in a long line, passing rocks to one another and eventually depositing them on a large mound that is growing outside of the barbican.

**Sleeara** and **3 guards** oversee this operation. The guards are callous, brutal, and quick to whip their fellows at any opportunity. One day, a guard may be whipped, and the next he is the one holding the whip.

Sleeara stalks around the dig, making sure the men are properly motivated. She has executed a few men for failure to meet her harsh expectations. Some of these men were staked out for the gargoyles, and one was thrown over the ledge. Sleeara's motivation is to press the men to complete the task before the end of the fortnight when the blood moon rises.

**Sleeara, Female Human Necromancer (MU10):** HP 34; AC 8[11] or 2[17] (missile) and 4[15] (melee) from *shield* spell; Atk *staff of power* (2d6) or *+1 dagger* (1d4+1); **Move** 12; **Save** 6 (+1, ring); AL C; **CL/XP** 11/1700; **Special:** +2 save vs. spells, wands and staffs, spells (4/4/3/2/2).
**Spells:** 1st—*charm person* (x2), *magic missile*, *shield*; 2nd—*detect good*, *ESP*, *invisibility*, *phantasmal force*; 3rd—*hold person*, *lightning bolt*, *suggestion*; 4th—*polymorph other*, *wall of ice*; 5th—*animate dead* (x2).
**Equipment:** *robe of wizardry*, *staff of power*, *+1 dagger*, *ring of protection +1*, pockets full of spell components.
**Note:** Sleeara hides her spellbook in her room in the Fest Haus.

**Guards, Male or Female Humans (3):** HD 4; HP 27, 23, 21; AC 5[14]; Atk polearm (1d8+1) or longbow x2 (1d6); **Move** 12; **Save** 13; AL N; **CL/XP** 4/120; **Special:** none. (*Monstrosities* 256) (see **Encounter I-B**)
**Equipment:** black enameled chainmail, white cape, polearm, longbow, 30 arrows, 1d4 gems (1d10x10 gp)

Sleeara is an overambitious brat. She believes she is vastly more powerful than she really is and goes to great lengths to prove her "superiority." Early in her short career, she fell in with Lord Raob, who at the time went under the name Raob Darkly. Although she no longer fancies him as much as she once did, he is still deeply infatuated with her. Sleeara, of course, has used his feelings to her advantage. She disposed of all competitors, such as a priestess of Demogorgon, and has solidified her position by discovering the history of the demon's amulet through her necromantic studies. Sleeara is likely to inquire about the characters' *portal rune* tattoo if they are captured. If possible, she tries to copy and use it. Sleeara goes to any length to impress someone, because doing so impresses herself.

## Encounter I-D: Raob and the Fest Haus (Area A-2)

The aboveground Fest Haus is a long and narrow structure that the dwarves once used presumably to host celebrations outside of the Citadel. It is made entirely of stone and has a simple opening as its entrance. Above the entrance, in an ancient dialect of Dwarven, an inscription reads "Festival House." The roof on the Fest Haus is of poor construction and tends to leak during rain. The interior of the structure is bare, except for the items Raob has moved into it.

Raob uses the Fest Haus as his base of operations. In fact, he pitched an elaborate red pavilion in the structure's center. Raob and Sleeara sleep in this pavilion (apart, much to Raob's chagrin). Raob's personal guards (the sergeants; see **Encounter I-B**) also sleep in the Fest Haus, but outside of the pavilion.

The pavilion itself has three "rooms." Two are the sleeping chambers, and one is a common area where Raob eats, dresses, and contemplates how he will rule the world once he obtains the demon's amulet. A large map of the known world is on the floor, with many of the country's names changed to "Skullcracker," "Raobland," or "Sleeara Hold." The map has a base value of 1,000 gp. There are also silk pillows, an incense burner, and a small mirror; together, these furnishings are worth 300 gp.

In Raob's sleeping chamber is an armor stand, a king-sized bed (which the guards still grumble about hauling up the Devil's Finger), and a stuffed bear missing a button eye hidden under the bed. The chamber also contains a chest, which is trapped with a **poisoned arrow** (save or die). Inside the chest are 10 platinum bars worth 1,000 gp each, a large ruby worth 250 gp, and an ancient cloth map showing the location of the Devil's Finger in the nearby mountain range.

In Sleeara's sleeping chamber are black silk blankets and a pillow. Underneath this bedroll is her spellbook. The spellbook contains all of the spells Sleeara currently has memorized; you can include additional spells as you see fit. The bedroll was a gift from Raob. A *warning cube* also rests on a small locked crate. The crate has been secured with a **lightning trap**, though nothing is inside the crate because Sleeara always carries her possessions with her. If activated, the lightning blast destroys the crate. The blast unleashes a 50-foot-long bolt that does 3d6 points of damage to anyone in its path unless they make a saving throw for half damage.

**Lord Raob Blackenheart, Male Human Warrior (Ftr12):** HP 70; AC 1[18]; **Atk** +2 *heavy flail* (1d8+8); **Move** 12; **Save** 4; **AL** C; **CL/XP** 12/2000; **Special:** multiple attacks (12) vs. creatures with 1 or fewer HD.

**Equipment:** +2 *plate mail*, helm, +2 *heavy flail*, *gauntlets of ogre power*.

Fully armed, Raob is an imposing sight. He wears black enameled full plate armor with a large helm bearing metal eagle's wings. A large open hand with an eye in the palm — Raob's symbol — is painted in gold on his breastplate. He usually has his helm open so he can bark orders at his men, showing his yellow teeth and grizzly beard.

Raob Blackenheart, a self-proclaimed lord with no ties to nobility, has the mewling personality of a four-year-old. Although clearly an adult, his basic motivations are similar to a young child's; he is moody, he loves to satisfy himself and his needs, and he hates anyone who stands in the way. He has a deep infatuation with Sleeara. This is the reason why he allows her to command him. Yet Raob may grow tired of her one day and eliminate her, as he has eliminated other concubines. Finally, Raob is a force of destruction. He is very large (standing 6 feet 5 inches tall and weighing over 250 pounds), with jet-black hair and a long black beard. His eyes dart around the room when anyone talks to him, as if he is always wary of an attack. He wields absolute control over his men due to the awe he strikes in them with his prowess in battle.

**Sergeants, Male or Female Humans (Ftr6) (8):** HD 6; HP 47, 45, 43, 41x2, 39, 37, 34; AC 5[14]; **Atk** bastard sword (1d8) or longbow x2 (1d6); **Move** 12; **Save** 9; **AL** C; **CL/XP** 6/400; **Special:** multiple attacks (5) vs. creatures with 1 or fewer HD. (see **Encounter I-B**)

**Equipment:** black chainmail, red cape, bastard sword, longbow, 30 arrows, 1d4 gems (1d10x10 gp).

Although he is fearful of magic and hates wizards (excluding Sleeara), Raob usually charges into the thick of any combat and calls out challenges to the largest of the enemy. While a few large battles have gone differently, Raob personally has never lost a challenge. With the cliff nearby, Raob may try to push someone over it to eliminate him or her. No tactic is beneath him. Raob commands his men as described in **Encounter II-B**.

# Encounter I-E: The Wheel House and Landing Area (Area A-3)

As previously mentioned, the Wheel House is a new building on the lower elevation on top of the Devil's Finger. It is a shanty-like wood structure crafted of odd pieces of brushwood hastily gathered far below.

The Wheel House hangs slightly over the cliff's edge. Inside the structure is a large and well-crafted wheel that functions as a spool for a very thick rope. The rope is connected by way of a pulley to a gigantic iron cauldron. Together, the entire system acts like an elevator.

At all times, three guards are far below watching the landing area; at night, they use torches to provide light for this operation. Above, the remaining eight guards work in shifts to turn the wheel, moving it around in a great circle. Operating the wheel requires at least two characters to make a successful Open Doors check; it usually takes three to four guards to turn the wheel. The remaining guards watch outside, always alert and present when the cauldron reaches the top. The cauldron weighs 200 pounds. If for any reason the cauldron is let loose and falls on top of someone, it deals 2d6 points of damage for every 10 feet it plummets, to a maximum of 20d6.

**Guards, Male or Female Humans (11):** HD 4; HP 31, 30, 29x3, 28, 27x4, 25; AC 5[14]; **Atk** polearm (1d8+1) or longbow x2 (1d6); **Move** 12; **Save** 13; **AL** N; **CL/XP** 4/120; **Special:** none. (*Monstrosities* 256) (see **Encounter I-B**)

**Equipment:** black enameled chainmail, white cape, polearm, longbow, 30 arrows, 1d4 gems (1d10x10 gp)



# Encounter I-F: Outer Barbican (Area A-4)

Like most of the Citadel, the outer barbican is nearly completely dilapidated. The great stone ceiling and towers are collapsed and crumbling. The Citadel is distinguished from the Devil's Finger because it has a brushed and smooth structure. Yet the Citadel has no visible entrance, except in the courtyard around the vault and the barbican.

The entrance to the Citadel through the barbican was formerly a 30-foot-wide entryway. This way has since been blocked by rubble. The dig nearby is concentrating on the west tower (**Area A-1**). The north tower is accessible from a collapsed wall on the north side. This collapsed wall has created a hole through which the characters could climb and enter the barbican.

Once inside, the characters enter a passageway in the north tower. The upper floors are destroyed. A number of rooms are in the north tower, but they are empty, with only bits of wood and dust (this area was once a barracks). In a corner room is a hole in the floor that has larger stones around its perimeter. This is not a privy, but rather access to a lower storage area. Through this storage area is the archway that gives the characters access to the Citadel (**Encounter I-J**). No guards patrol here.

# Encounter I-G: The Vault (Area A-5)

The vault is a very large cube of obsidian, each side flawless and mirror-like black stone. Around the edges is a crater that was smoothed by the Citadel's architects. Only 50 feet of the cube is visible from the surface, but it extends another 16 feet into the granite. Only the key provides access into the vault, as described in **Chapter Six**.

Around the vault is a low, five-foot-high wall that forms a pentagram. The wall is made of individual stones and has crumbled and fallen in places. Each individual stone has the same dwarven rune on it; the rune reads "evil" and is non-magical.

There is no way into the Citadel itself, since it is a façade. The outer Citadel was dug out of the granite below. Theoretically, a party could blast its way down 40 to 50 feet, as Raob did; however, this strategy is mere folly and a waste of valuable time. The vault radiates strong evil and overwhelming magic.

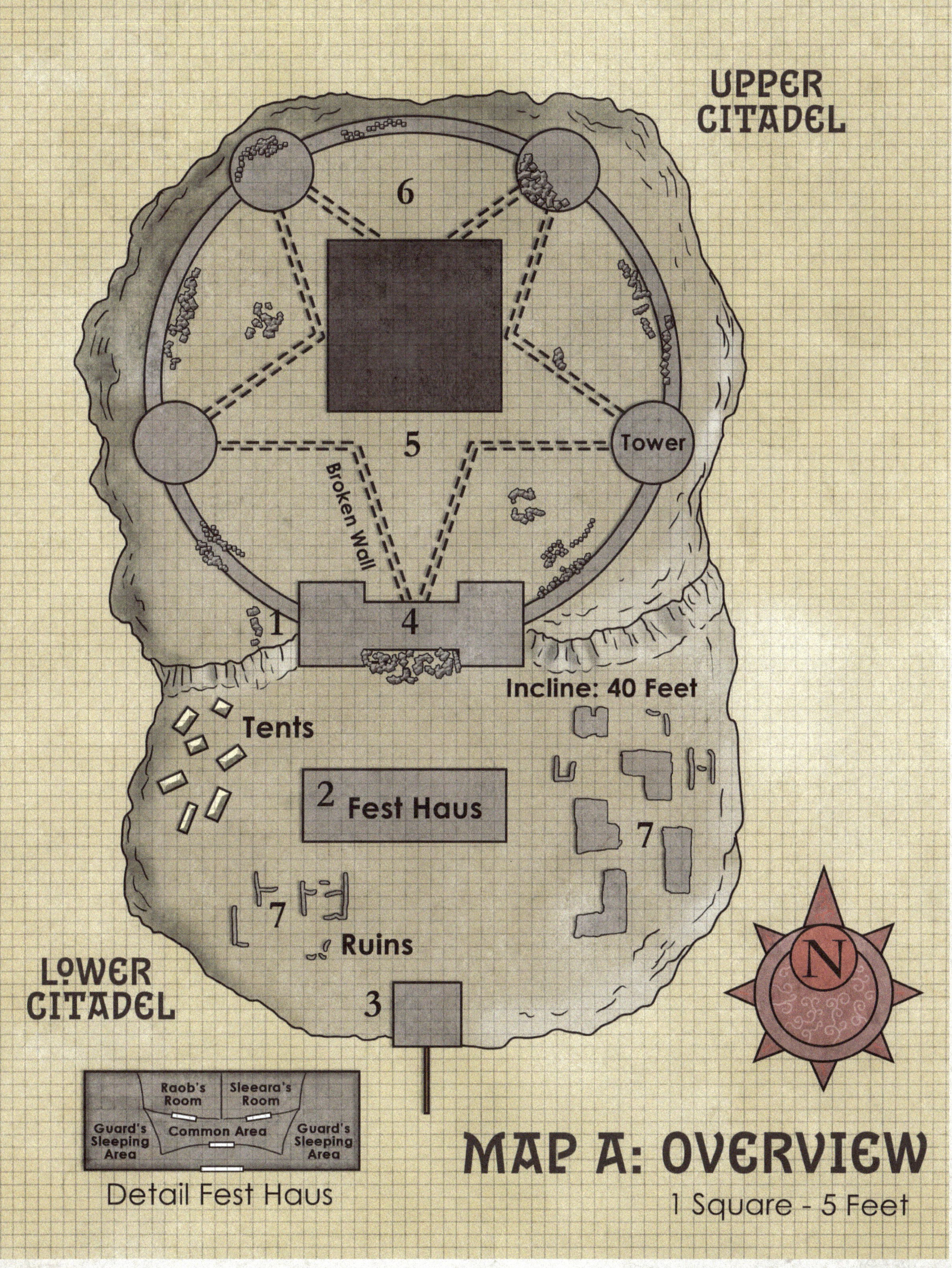

UPPER CITADEL
6
5
Tower
Broken Wall
1
4
Incline: 40 Feet
Tents
2 Fest Haus
7
7
Ruins
3
LOWER CITADEL
N
Raob's Room
Sleeara's Room
Guard's Sleeping Area
Common Area
Guard's Sleeping Area
Detail Fest Haus
MAP A: OVERVIEW
1 Square - 5 Feet

## Encounter I-H: The Upper Citadel (Area A-6)

The old remnants of the Citadel's towers and walls barely stand. The wall was made of individual bricks of granite that fit together without mortar. This is an example of the unique and marvelous structure that the dwarves created. When it was first built, the wall formed a circle and was 50 feet high and five feet wide. Now, large holes show in the wall where the bricks were toppled over.

The large, 70-foot-tall towers are also nearly all collapsed. Some are mere rings, and at least one retains part of its crenulations (like the wall, it was made of granite bricks). The party can explore the towers, but the only entrance to the Citadel below is through the barbican (**Encounter I-F**).

## Encounter I-I: Outer Buildings (Area A-7)

Like the Fest Haus, these buildings were made of large slabs of granite stacked together. Whatever occupied the interior has long since turned to dust or been removed. The original purpose of these buildings is unknown.

The buildings are somewhat unstable. Combat or some other such activity has a 10% chance of toppling a structure. If this event occurs, a character must succeed at a saving throw to avoid suffering 3d6 points of damage from falling rubble.

## Encounter I-J: Entry to Chaos

The corner room of the lower barbican leads to a great archway that is carved with numerous ancient dwarven runes inlaid with brass. Rubble and rock lie five feet beyond the archway. Near the archway, the ribcage of a dwarf is propped up against the wall, the rusted blade of a dagger lying within it. A few rats make their home in a corner rubble pile.

The characters can activate the portal merely by walking through it if they wear the *portal rune*. Anyone else present described in **Chapter One** — other than Sleeara — would be too perplexed or frightened to attempt to follow the characters. If anyone does and fails to possess a *portal rune*, he or she is transported through time and considered lost (the exact location is up to you, although a time when the characters' home planet has long since been destroyed — and thus the unfortunate is transported to a vacuum — or when the entire planet is covered in primal molten rock are good choices).

If Sleeara is secretly observing the characters, she may immediately realize the truth of the archway and the necessary rune. If she saw such a rune on a character's neck, she is likely to follow them (as described in **Chapter Two**) once she inscribes and tattoos the rune on herself.

When the characters move through the archway, they are instantly transported to the "Siege of Orcus" in **Chapter Three**. The rubble is gone, the area is changed, and the silence is soon broken by the sounds of dwarven battle cries resonating through the halls.

If the characters look through the archway back toward the direction from which they entered, they see blackness. In other words, when standing in the archway during the "Siege of Orcus," the characters do not see the broken stone and collapsed barbican from which they entered. Instead, they see inky blackness and apparent nothingness.

# CHAPTER TWO:
# THE CITADEL

Chaos. Total chaos. This is the path the characters select. This is the path you must arbitrate. What follows is bizarre, unusual, and — with preparation by you — thoroughly fun.

This chapter first explains a general outline for the characters' adventures in the Citadel. Next is a description of and motivations for "competing" NPC parties. Although whether to include these parties in **Chaos Rising** is up to you, doing so is ultimately a wise idea. Finally, this chapter includes a description of the Citadel's two levels. Since the Citadel is mostly unchanged, the two times the characters move through it, these descriptions are provided here. Further specifics are explained in the pertinent chapters, **Chapter Three: Descent — The Siege of Orcus** and **Chapter Five: Ascent — Necromantic Dreams**.

## A Journey Through Chaos

In Stage Two, the characters time travel. They leave the present and enter the Citadel through the upper archway. In doing so, they enter an alternate demiplane that occupies only two levels of the Citadel. The laws of physics on the demiplane are the same as the characters' home plane, and time advances at the same rate. In other words, the dwarves on the demiplane age and die the same as dwarves on the home plane. Practically nothing is different except that the barbican portal can access only the demiplane.

Once through the archway, the characters are thrust into the middle of a battle. Orcus has persuaded an evil dwarven priest, Kinst, to open a special gate into the Citadel, bypassing all its defenses. The dwarven high priest, Usis, received a vision two days before the attack. In this vision, Usis saw demons devouring dwarves within the Citadel. Usis warned King Galm, the Clan Flammeaxte leader, and together they prepared for the assault.

During the preparations, Usis fell into a coma due to Kinst poisoning him one day before the characters' arrival. No one suspects Kinst and believes that the poisoning is the work of demons. Undeterred, King Galm prepares patrols and believes that the demons might arrive through the upper portal.

As the characters enter the upper portal, they are met by a group of guardian dwarves. The characters must do some quick explaining and possibly show the *portal rune* they used to gain access to the Citadel. If the characters gain these dwarves' trust, they are escorted to King Galm, who then interrogates them. Galm wants to know why they are in the Citadel and how they gained access; he should at best be skeptical during this conversation.

Toward the end of the conversation, King Galm is alerted that demons are within the Citadel and running amok. Galm immediately wants to join the battle. His advisors restrain him, however, and warn that if he should fall and the demons acquire his *portal rune*, the enemy will gain access to the catacombs. An advisor to Galm — or perhaps Galm himself — suggests that the characters take care of the threat as a sign of their good intentions. This suggestion triggers a whirlwind of events that is more fully described in **Chapter Four**.

Assuming that the characters persuade King Galm to give them the *portal rune* to the catacombs, which might be inscribed by the priests of Dwurfater from the rune of the back of Galm's neck, they enter the catacombs' demiplane. Like the Citadel, the catacombs are similar physically and temporally to the characters' home plane. Yet the catacombs the characters enter are at a different era than the "Siege of Orcus": they are in the present — or, the same time that the characters left behind when they entered the Citadel.

Once in the catacombs, the characters must overcome guardians and traps to retrieve the key. The key is unusual in many respects. One such property is that the key suppresses magic as per an *anti-magic shell*. This property does not prevent the characters from using the *portal key* to return from the catacombs and re-enter the Citadel's demiplane. The *portal key*, as explained in **Chapter One**, actually functions in an *anti-magic shell*. Yet it does not return the characters to the time of Galm, where they are likely heroes. Instead, the *portal key* takes them to "Necromantic Dreams" (see **Chapter Five**).

In "Necromantic Dreams," the Citadel is completely abandoned. A priest (Giltz, now a dark custodian) led his army into the Citadel in search of the key. While his army was successful, Giltz died in a suicide effort by the last defenders. These events occurred more than 100 years before the characters arrive the via the lower portal.

The remnants of Giltz's army, the undead, roam the Citadel. The entire complex is dark and seems barely disturbed; thrones sit empty and benches gather dust. Although the Citadel was attacked, the interior is oddly in the same condition as when the characters left the "Siege of Orcus" … as if the dwarves suddenly disappeared and were replaced with undead. The characters must make their way through this nightmarish Citadel and return to their home plane through the upper archway. Unfortunately for them, Giltz has other plans.

In both the "Siege of Orcus" and the return trip through "Necromantic Dreams," the characters cannot leave the demiplane without going through the upper or lower portal. Any attempt to leave the upper or lower levels via *teleportation* or similar means is stunted by the Citadel's magical wards. The Citadel was designed with magical protections imbued into the fabric of the structure or plane to stop any evil-aligned entity from entering it via a *gate* or other magical means (note, however, that Orcus overcame these wards by using a specially-crafted magic item). *Teleport* and similar spells *within* the levels are permissible. In other words, the characters may *teleport* between rooms they are familiar with inside the Citadel. They cannot *teleport* outside the Citadel. Furthermore, the Citadel's demiplane is infused with dwarven magical energy that repairs any attempt to break through the Citadel's walls.

Overcoming Giltz, the characters return to their home plane. Here, the final chapter begins. The characters discover that while they entered the demiplanes of the Citadel and the catacombs, time moved very shortly in the outside world (perhaps one day for every four the characters experienced) — giving them time to deal with Raob (if necessary) and use the key when the blood moon rises. With preparation, you can easily play these chaotic events as described above.

## Competing NPCs (Time Travelers)

Recommended, but not necessary, is the addition of an unexpected challenge. The characters might assume that they will meet guardians and traps. They might not foresee others seeking to take the key.

These competing NPCs might enter the Citadel during the "Siege of Orcus" or "Necromantic Dreams" and challenge the characters. This challenge could be to beat the characters into the catacombs during the "Siege of Orcus", or it could be to take the key while the characters are in "Necromantic Dreams."

Below are three groups of NPCs and a single NPC "operative": the Brotherhood of Ooze, the Cabal of the Beard, the Silvereyes, and the nefarious mercenary Imbo the Undying. With the exception of the Cabal, any of these NPCs may be inserted in either the "Siege of Orcus" or "Necromantic Dreams."

Use these groups with caution. To be certain, this adventure is not easy. Thus, the NPCs should be inserted with a specific plan in mind, as each group employs different tactics.

For simplicity's sake, using only a couple of the NPC groups in either time period might prove more effective. For example, use Imbo the Undying during the "Siege of Orcus" and the Brotherhood of the Ooze along with the Cabal of the Beard during "Necromantic Dreams." Still, a fun challenge might be to arbitrate two such groups at the same time against the characters. The characters might find themselves allying with one against another. Switching allegiances or joining together against a common foe such as Kinst, these NPCs provide unique challenges for the party beyond the norm.

When introducing the NPCs, having the NPCs fight the denizens of whichever era you place them in "behind the scenes" may be too difficult. Instead, simply place the NPCs in a set locale and consider that they fought or made their way there by eliminating other creatures not described. This way, the NPCs become a living entity from the encounter point forward in harrying the characters and their quest.

Also, with the exception of the Brotherhood of Ooze, the NPCs are not illogical or dim. They are some of the finest warriors, priests, and wizards who, just like the characters, are after a prize of considerable value. They might leave the Citadel and return later (such as leave in the "Siege of Orcus" and return in "Necromantic Dreams"). Or they might leave and attempt to ambush the characters in the characters' real world. Also, these NPCs could ambush the characters after the events of this adventure take place as the characters attempt to return the demon's amulet to their benefactor. Finally, these NPCs might even become a reoccurring enemy in your campaign world long after **Chaos Rising**.

### The Cabal of the Beard

The Cabal of the Beard is a group of dwarven guardians established in the Citadel hundreds of years after the "Siege of Orcus." These guardians believe that King Galm of old made a horrendous mistake in allowing the characters to enter the catacombs. Over the years, the cabal grew strong and opposed the ruling king. Successful in their coup, the cabal sends Bertram and company through time to take the key from the characters. Interestingly, the rise of the cabal is directly responsible for the success of Kinst later in time owing to the divisions it caused within Clan Flammeaxte.

The Cabal of the Beard should be used only in "Necromantic Dreams." The cabal is perplexed that the Citadel is in ruins and is only discovering the truth that the dwarves have all perished. This realization causes much sadness to the cabal, which, although Lawful, is likely to blame the characters for the death of their people.

The leader of the cabal is Bertram, who is arrogant and foolish. The rest of these dwarves are not as foolish and do not likely risk their lives fighting a foe that they recognize as having good intentions. Thus, a parley is possible, especially if a good-aligned dwarf leads or appears to lead the party.

All of the cabal have a *portal rune* to enter the upper hall. Instead of taking them to the outer world, it returns them to their time era.

Encountering the cabal is an excellent opportunity for the characters to gain allies to help them defeat some of the more difficult foes in "Necromantic Dreams." These dwarves are skeptical and have large chips on their shoulders (for dwarves); they are likely to attack, retreat, and assess the situation. An initial encounter will not likely lead to death, as far as the cabal is concerned. What the characters do is another story.

If the party does not include a dwarf, the characters may have difficulty explaining why they are carrying a 500-pound platinum anvil. The cabal, like almost all dwarves of the Citadel at any time, has never seen the key and is unlikely to recognize it as such. If the characters tell the cabal that the anvil is the key, however, a battle to the death is very likely.

Even with a dwarf in the party, unless the words "holy quest" or some similar dire reason is quickly explained, the cabal may become hostile. A good way for the characters to gain the cabal's assistance is to implore their help and ask for guidance through the Citadel. The cabal may view this as a redeeming opportunity and be happy to oblige.

The cabal is immediately hostile if the characters are in the company of the Brotherhood of Ooze. The cabal knows little of the brotherhood but can tell immediately that they serve chaos and the Faceless Lord, the defeated foe of Dwurfater.

The following description details the cabal. Its use is a matter of your discretion.

---

This entire room is full of rubble, trash, and splintered wood. Where once the dwarves of the Citadel lived is now destruction and decay.

Four dwarves stand among the junk. One wears a dwarven-sized suit of silvery plate armor that has an otherworldly glow from the magical light his group is using. He has a tuft of red whiskers below a full helm and a mask of a jolly dwarf face with the wearer's beard and lower chin uncovered. The dwarf holds a large battleaxe. Next to him stands a shorter dwarf in the same style of armor. Obviously a female, she presses her lips together as if ready to blurt something out; she holds an oversized warhammer with a gleaming silver head. Behind them, balanced on a plank of wood sticking out of the junk pile, is a very thin and raven-haired dwarf, smiling broadly. This dwarf begins to snicker, slowly twirling a quarterstaff.

Finally, at the base of the junk pile is a filthy dwarf wearing a tattered cloak over rust-spotted armor. He has a large scar across his face that ends in a gap between his teeth. His bristly red hair and beard are unkempt. He hefts a large scythe and braces as if to swing it.

The first dwarf says to you, "The deceivers! Come, me brudders, let us have our taste of sweet vengeance!"

---

**Lord Bertram auth'Tanak, Male Dwarf Cabal of the Beard, Follower of Dwurfater (Ftr8):** HP 58; AC 0[19]; **Atk** *+2 battleaxe* (1d8+8) or sling (1d4 [+1 with *+1 bullet*]); **Move** 9; **Save** 5 (+2, ring); **AL** N; **CL/XP** 8/800; **Special:** +4 save vs. magic, darkvision (60ft), multiple attacks (8) vs. creatures with 1 or fewer HD.
**Equipment:** plate mail, large steel shield, *+2 battleaxe*, sling, 30 *+1 bullets*, *gauntlets of ogre power*, *ring of protection +2*, *potion of animal control*, *potion of growth*, *potion of heroism*, *potion of invulnerability*.
*Description:* Bertram appears as a squat suit of pristine armor with a tuft of red whiskers billowing from his chin. He is never without his family's great heirloom: a battleaxe dating back to the time of the Citadel's founding. He is harsh and is incredibly bigoted against all non-dwarves.
*Background:* Bertram is the direct descendant of a coward who hid during the "Siege of Orcus." This dwarf was so consumed by guilt that he swore that one day a descendent of his would make up for his cowardice. Bertram knows this story and is fanatical about protecting the Citadel.
*Motivation:* Bertram had little interest in the cabal until he received the vision from Dwurfater. As an elder of the cabal, he is a zealot through and through. Bertram has trained his group hard and accepts nothing less than total victory.

## DWURFATER

**Alignment:** Lawful
**Areas of Influence:** Earth, Good, Strength
**Typical Worshippers:** Dwarves (good-aligned)
**Symbol:** Hammer and anvil
**Favored Weapon:** Warhammer

Dwurfater is the father of all dwarves. He eternally works his forge to create dwarves to populate the universe so that they can glorify him with works of mithral and steel.

**Kunuld, Female Dwarf Cabal of the Beard, Priestess of Dwurfater (Clr8):** HP 40; AC 2[17]; **Atk** *+1 warhammer* (1d4+1); **Move** 9; **Save** 8; **AL** N; **CL/XP** 8/800; **Special:** +2 save vs. paralyzation and poison, +4 save vs. magic, banish undead, darkvision (60ft), spells (2/2/2/2/2).
**Spells:** 1st—*cure light wounds, protection from evil;* 2nd—*bless, find traps;* 3rd—*prayer, remove curse;* 4th—*create water, cure serious wounds;* 5th—*dispel evil, raise dead.*
**Equipment:** plate mail armor, small shield, *+1 warhammer, potion of clairvoyance, potion of healing,* scroll (*cure serious wounds, neutralize poison*), scroll (*commune, raise dead*).
*Description:* Kunuld is a devotee of Dwurfater. Like Bertram, she wears gleaming plate armor. Beneath the armor, she has a pleasant, plump face and a smiling disposition. Kunuld is a kind person but does not flinch from a chance to smite evil.
*Background:* Kunuld was born into the priesthood of Dwurfater. She has dedicated her life to his cause and is delighted that Bertram selected her for this holy mission.
*Motivation:* Kunuld worries that Bertram's fervor will be his undoing. She is levelheaded and will be one of the first to attempt to parley with the characters if possible.
**Teera auth'Narak, Female Dwarf Cabal of the Beard (Thf7):** HP 23; AC 5[14]; **Atk** *+1 staff* (1d6+1) or dagger (1d4) or light crossbow (1d4+1); **Move** 9; **Save** 9 (+2, armor); **AL** L; **CL/XP** 7/600; **Special:** +2 save bonus vs. traps and magical devices, +4 save vs. magic, backstab (x3), darkvision (60ft), read languages, thieving skills.
**Thieving Skills:** Climb 91%, Tasks/Traps 55%, Hear 5 in 6, Hide 45%, Silent 55%, Locks 45%.
**Equipment:** *+2 leather armor, +1 staff,* dagger, light crossbow, 21 bolts, *ring of fire resistance.*
*Description:* Teera is a thin dwarf with flowing, raven-colored hair. She almost always has a smile on her face and loves the thrill of adventure. Teera tends to annoy others because of her shrill voice and laughter. She wears oversized (elf-sized) leather armor that she keeps well-oiled. Also, she uses an unusual weapon for a dwarf: the quarterstaff.
*Background:* Teera always longed to leave the Citadel and explore the outside world. Yet her father prohibited such wanderlust. As a youth, the elves — the dwarves' ancient enemy — fascinated her. Although she never met one, reading about their carefree lifestyle and troublemaking suited her. Bertram was smitten with her and still bears feelings for her. Teera has always thought of Bertram as stuffy, but she is very loyal to him.
*Motivation:* Teera lives for adventure. She secretly fancies herself an elf soul (a being with the soul of the elf, but who is actually something else). She sticks with Bertram as long as the arrangement suits her; however, if a situation gets very dangerous or deadly, she may sneak off.
**Auran, Male Dwarf Cabal of the Beard (Ftr9):** HP 66; AC 2[17]; **Atk** *+1 scythe* (1d8+1) or light crossbow (1d4+1 [+2 with *+1 bolt*]); **Move** 9; **Save** 5 (+1, cloak); **AL** N; **CL/XP** 9/1100; **Special:** +4 save vs. magic, darkvision (60ft), multiple attacks (9) vs. creatures with 1 or fewer HD.
**Equipment:** chainmail, raggedy cloak, *+1 large steel shield, +1 scythe,* light crossbow, 30 bolts, 15 *+1 bolts, cloak of protection +1.*
*Description:* Auran is an incredibly hairy dwarf. With the exception of his cheekbones, nose, and eyes, Auran has brown hair covering his entire face. He rarely speaks, but when he does, he usually barks out insults and threats. He wears a raggedy old cloak over armor that squeaks a bit too much. He is very fond of his scythe ("Cutting the chaff of life" is a favorite expression) and his shield emblazoned with Dwurfater's symbol (a hammer and anvil).
*Background:* Auran is an old friend of Bertram's, but he does not trust the other dwarf's leadership. He was regimented to learn to be a guard while his noble-born friend Bertram was privileged to learn better fighting tactics. In addition to his station in the Citadel during the time from which they came, Auran feels everyone picks on him as he had a very difficult childhood.

*Motivation:* Auran is a very bitter dwarf with little patience for folly. Like Bertram, he is secretly infatuated with Teera, which explains how he can stand her "shenanigans." Auran does not trust any of the bigger people (humans, elves, orcs) he has read about, and due to the stories he has read, he usually displays an open disdain for the smaller people (halflings). Auran is likely to lead the group if Bertram is killed.

**Sample Tactics:** If combat becomes necessary, the cabal springs into action. Bertram drinks a *potion of growth* and immediately bellows challenges at the enemy. He then engages them. Auran attempts to move to the back of the enemies' position and uses his massive scythe on enemy casters, hopefully flanking the frontlines of the enemy fighters. Teera fires her crossbow while protecting Kunuld. Kunuld's tactics change depending on the encounter, though her primary role is to heal and support her comrades.

## THE BROTHERHOOD OF THE OOZE

The Brotherhood of the Ooze is a bumbling and absentminded group dedicated to the worship of absolute chaos. Sickly and vile, a Brother of the Ooze makes his way through life seeding chaos wherever he roams. A Brother is the personification of chaos. He tries to bring disorder to order, disharmony to harmony, and is thoroughly evil.

Drawing both men and women, the Brotherhood of the Ooze has no sexism save the name. The Brothers of the Ooze are mostly clerics and some magic-users. They learn the art of chaos, and this path leads them to the name of the Faceless Lord.

Brothers of the Ooze cling together. They are outcasts, the downtrodden, and those with darkened hearts. Although a Brother might be found in any locale, the group recruits in beggar quarters in large cities and in deep underground temples where they perform horrific rites and delight in the perfection of chaos — the oozes.

Through the direction of their master, the Faceless Lord, they preach and chant litanies on the virtues of sludge and muck. Slime is chaos perfected to the Brotherhood: it is ever-flowing, ever-moving, and its effects are unpredictable.

One way you may use the brotherhood is to make them comical, as per the below description. A group that is chanting about the glory of sludge while sliding about on their own slime is humorous in its own way. The humor vanishes, however, when these comical antics end in a deadly encounter.

The brotherhood made a pilgrimage to the Devil's Finger to discover more about their obscure religion. Since the Faceless Lord's imprisonment within the vault, his powers as a deity have greatly diminished. Although the Faceless Lord is faintly aware of the brotherhood and how pathetic they are, he believes that they could also be his salvation. In a vision, he sent the brotherhood the image of the *portal rune*. After a week of debate, someone figured out what the *portal rune* meant and the brotherhood entered the Citadel.

If the characters have the key, the brotherhood attempts to take it from them and leave the Citadel. Such an outcome could effectively end the adventure, so the encounter must be judged very carefully.

---

Down the hallway, you hear shouts and angry intonations. Suddenly, a group of people turns the corner. They are engaged in deep conversation and are pushing one another into the wall. Above them floats a magical light.

"I still believe that the primordial order of all things begins with ooze," says one of the men. He is a gigantic blob of a person. He wears a stained and greasy night shirt, has long gray hair down the middle of his back, and gigantic bags droop under his fleshy eyes.

"What are you talking about, Sludgebearer?" a woman responds. "You just said *order*. What do you know about the purity of the ooze if you used the word *order* in the same breath?" She pushes the obese blob into a wall, making a loud slap of flesh against stone. Her long dark hair has not seen a comb in at least a decade, and her skin looks rotted. She wears a simple purple tunic that is badly in need of repair. Without warning, the woman begins to retch and looks as if she will be sick.

"Shut up, Slimetalker," speaks the group's tallest member. "You are obviously still addled — the truth of chaos is embodied within the ever-changing perfection of slime." The man wears a heavy brown robe. He has a vulture-like neck and an enormous mole at the end of the crooked nose. Leaning on a twisted piece of black wood as he walks, the man seems to be sweating profusely.

"Quagmire, if I may say something," asks a similarly robed man. This member of the group has no hair at all, and his skin is heavily wrinkled and covered in thick, viscous goo.

"No, you may not," Quagmire says, taking a slow jab at the smaller man with his staff. The other man jumps out of the way, which causes the final member of their group trip over him.

Jumping to her feet, the thick and squat woman with short-cropped hair points in your general direction. Wearing a nearly transparent pink robe that reveals, among other things, boils all over her body, the woman seems otherwise unarmed. She shouts, "Look!"

The entire group falls silent, staring at you with narrowing eyes.

---

**Quagmire, Male Human Brother of the Ooze, Priest of Jubilex (Clr7):** HP 49; AC 7[12]; Atk *+2 flail* (1d8+2); Move 12; Save 9; AL C; CL/XP 9/1100; **Special:** +1 save vs. charm, confusion and fear spells, +2 save vs. paralyzation and poison, banish undead and oozes, litany of chaos (3/day, chant confuses enemies, save or stand confused for 1d4 rounds), ooze armor (+2 AC bonus, excretes from pores, similar to phlegm in color and consistency), purity of slime (1/day, summon ooze, 35% chance [5% chance per level]; roll 1d6: 1–2, grey ooze; 3–4, crystal ooze; 5–6, black pudding), spells (2/2/2/1/1), summon lesser ooze demon (1/week, 14% chance [2% chance per level], serves for 1 hour).

**Spells:** 1st—*cure light wounds, green water**; 2nd—*bless, find traps*; 3rd—*muck**, *remove curse*; 4th—*cure serious wounds, mucus mask**; 5th—*dispel evil, slime bucket**.

**Equipment:** robes, *+2 morningstar, potion of healing, potion of extra healing, staff of sludge**, 2d8 gems (1d4 x 100 gp).

* see **Appendix A: New Magic**.

*Description:* Quagmire is a tall and lanky man. He has an enormous mole on the end of a crooked nose, and tufts of bristly brown hair sprout sporadically around his egg-shaped head. Quagmire wears the long thick brown robes of his order and leans on the twisted *staff of sludge* (see sidebar). His appearance is not nearly as nasty as his horrific personality — for he is sadistic and self-loathing. Quagmire is the quintessential grumpy leader.

*Background:* Quagmire — even he doesn't remember his original name — was once a sculptor. For years he tried to create a perfect sculpture of a paramour. Although his skills were strong, he was never satisfied with his results. Eventually, he made a pact with the Faceless Lord to give him the ability to accomplish this task. In exchange for the ability, Quagmire devoted his soul to the demon. The Faceless Lord turned the sculptor's beloved into stone and tricked Quagmire into believing that he had accomplished the task. When Quagmire discovered his folly, he grew mad with rage and lost his sanity. Now, many years later, his hatred of his master has spurred Quagmire to devote himself faithfully to the Faceless Lord in the hope that the Faceless Lord will destroy him and allow him the death for which he yearns. Unfortunately, the Faceless Lord finds the tormented life of Quagmire humorous and amusing.

*Motivation:* Quagmire is the leader of the brotherhood because he has served the Faceless Lord the longest and can yell the loudest. He believes that the Faceless Lord has sent the brotherhood on a suicide mission to retrieve the key. He relishes the opportunity to meet his end; however, he will not act foolishly.

## STAFF

### STAFF OF SLUDGE

This unusual staff is a favorite among the twisted followers of the Faceless Lord because of its ability to summon oozes. This long, wooden staff is knotted and twisted, and it seeps and pumps out a green ichor as if it were a living being. It can call forth an ooze three times per day. Yet there is a chance every time the staff is used that the wielder is reduced to a puddle of muck. The oozes summoned are as follows (roll 1d12):

| 1d12 | Summoned Ooze |
| --- | --- |
| 1–2 | green slime |
| 3–5 | grey ooze |
| 6–7 | ochre jelly |
| 8–10 | gelatinous cube |
| 11 | black pudding |
| 12 | The user must succeed at a saving throw or be reduced to a puddle of green slime. All non-stone possessions are immediately destroyed. |

**Sludgebearer, Male Human Brother of the Ooze (Mnk6):** HP 19; AC 2[17]; **Atk** 2 strikes (1d12) or wooden sword (1d6+3); **Move** 17; **Save** 10; **AL** C; **CL/XP** 8/800; **Special:** +1 save vs. charm, confusion and fear spells, +2 save vs. paralysis and poison, +3 weapon damage bonus, alertness (1-in-6 chance of being surprised), deadly strike (when attack roll is 5 higher than needed, 75% chance to be stunned for 2d6 rounds, 25% chance to kill enemy), deflect missiles (saving throw), heal self (1d6+1 hit points per day), litany of chaos (3/day, chant confuses enemies, save or stand confused for 1d4 rounds), multiple attacks, slow falling (fall 20ft with no damage if near wall), ooze armor (+2 AC bonus, excretes from pores, similar to phlegm in color and consistency), purity of slime (1/day, summon ooze, 30% chance [5% chance per level]; roll 1d6: 1–2, grey ooze; 3–4, crystal ooze; 5–6, black pudding), summon lesser ooze demon (1/week, 12% chance [2% chance per level], serves for 1 hour), thieving skills, speak with animals.
**Thieving Skills:** Climb 90%, Tasks/Traps 40%, Hear 4 in 6, Hide 35%, Silent 45%, Locks 35%.
**Equipment:** simple robes, wooden sword, *potion of healing*.
*Description:* Sludgebearer is a disgusting, obese blob of a person. Looks are deceiving, though, as he can use the morass of slime about him to move with amazing speed. Instead of the long brown robes of his brothers, he wears a greasy nightshirt and cap. Sludgebearer also has long, greasy gray hair and sunken eyes. He rarely speaks.
*Background:* Once a good-aligned monk, Sludgebearer now barely remembers his name and the name of the deity to whom he was devoted. Sludgebearer long ago committed a grave sin that turned him from the light. Finding solace in food, he quickly became a glutton. Quagmire found him in this state and recruited him for the brotherhood.
*Motivation:* Sludgebearer cares not for his fellow brothers. He simply desires to kill as a means of striking out at a world that turned its back on him. Sludgebearer has a deep-seated hate for Quagmire due to his years serving with him.
**Slimetalker, Female Human Brother of the Ooze Magic-User (MU9):** HP 30; AC 7[12] or 2[17] (missile) and 4[15] (melee) from *shield* spell; **Atk** *+1 dagger* (1d4+1); **Move** 12; **Save** 5 (+2, ring); **AL** C; **CL/XP** 11/1700; **Special:** +1 save vs. charm, confusion and fear spells, +2 save vs. spells, wands and staffs, litany of chaos (3/day, chant confuses enemies, save or stand confused for 1d4 rounds), ooze armor (+2 AC bonus, excretes from pores, similar to phlegm in color and consistency), purity of slime (1/day, summon ooze, 45% chance [5% chance per level]; roll 1d6: 1–2, grey ooze; 3–4, crystal ooze; 5–6, black pudding], summon lesser ooze demon (1/week, 18% chance [2% chance per level], serves for 1 hour), spells (4/3/3/2/1).
**Spells:** 1st—*charm person* (x2), *magic missile*, *shield*; 2nd—*detect good, invisibility, ooze bolt*, phantasmal force*; 3rd—*hold person, lightning bolt, slimeball**; 4th—*mucus mask, polymorph other*; 5th—*animate dead* (x2).
**Equipment:** simple wool tunic, *+1 dagger*, jug of the *liquor of vomit* (see sidebar), *ring of protection +2*, scroll (*rot to the core**), scroll

---

(*polymorph self*, gelatinous cube shape only), spellbook, 5d4 gems (1d4 x 100 gp). * see **Appendix A: New Magic**.
*Description:* Slimetalker is short and fair, with long dark hair in knots and tangles. She wears a simple purple tunic showing off her bruised and torn skin. She always expresses an opinion, but follows whoever is in charge of the brotherhood.
*Background:* Slimetalker is a former spy for the church of a Lawful deity. She was charged with infiltrating the brotherhood and determining the level of threat it posed. Unfortunately, her ruse was discovered, and she was forced to drink a strange sludge concoction: the *liquor of vomit* (see sidebar). The drink made her thoroughly evil, and to this day she is prone to vomit at inopportune times as a result of imbibing the potion.
*Motivation:* Slimetalker speaks in between belches. She willingly serves the brotherhood as a mindless zealot. Only a *wish* can cure her condition.

---

## THE FACELESS LORD

**Alignment:** Chaotic evil.
**Areas of Influence:** Chaos, Slimes.
**Typical Worshippers:** Humans (insane; usually males).
**Symbol:** A splatter mark with a red eye in the center.
**Favored Weapon:** Flail (The Pulper).

The Faceless Lord is a demon prince sometimes worshipped as a deity. He is chaos personified. Also thoroughly evil, he strives to slow chaos and discord among the planes. He is most often depicted as an enormous and amorphous blob that spews forth foul and sickly slimes of many colors.

---

**Muckcreeper, Male Human Brother of the Ooze (Thf7):** HP 25; AC 7[12]; **Atk** *+1 electrical short sword* (1d6+1 + 1d6 electricity) or *+1 dagger* (1d4+1); **Move** 12; **Save** 9; **AL** C; **CL/XP** 9/1100; **Special:** +1 save vs. charm, confusion and fear spells, +2 save bonus vs. traps and magical devices, backstab (x3), litany of chaos (3/day, chant confuses enemies, save or stand confused for 1d4 rounds), ooze armor (+2 AC bonus, excretes from pores, similar to phlegm in color and consistency), purity of slime (1/day, summon ooze, 35% chance [5% chance per level]; roll 1d6: 1–2, grey ooze; 3–4, crystal ooze; 5–6, black pudding), read languages, summon lesser ooze demon (1/week, 14% chance [2% chance per level], serves for 1 hour)thieving skills.
**Thieving Skills:** Climb 91%, Tasks/Traps 45%, Hear 5 in 6, Hide 40%, Silent 50%, Locks 40%.
**Equipment:** robes, *+1 electrical short sword, +2 dagger, potion of healing, potion of invisibility*, 3 vials of giant wasp poison (save or paralyzed for 2d6 rounds), 5d4 gems (1d4 x 100 gp),
*Description:* Muckcreeper is short, and his face is heavily scarred from acid. Like Quagmire, he wears the robes of the brotherhood. He has no hair at all. His skin is heavily wrinkled from prolonged exposure to the prismatic slime that seeps from his skin. Muckcreeper is talkative but prefers talking to his sword above anyone else.
*Background:* Muckcreeper was a street urchin whom Quagmire took as a slave. Muckcreeper grew to hate Quagmire. Still, he took his licks and learned to appreciate the chaos that the brotherhood seeds throughout the world.
*Motivation:* Muckcreeper believes that he is almost ready to lead. Unlike Quagmire, he is fully devoted to the utter chaos that the Faceless Lord represents. Thus, Muckcreeper is biding his time before he takes over the brotherhood. He truly puts his heart into his work and revels in the blood of his victims. Muckcreeper is the most likely to run and escape from an encounter with the characters.

---

## LIQUOR OF VOMIT

The *liquor of vomit* is a horrific brew. It has the consistency of mucus, the color of pus, and the odor of the dirtiest troglodyte in all of creation. Once imbibed, the brew curses the drinker, although a successful saving throw negates the effects. The alignment of the imbiber is radically altered to Chaotic. The alteration is mental as well as moral, and the individual changed by the *liquor of vomit* thoroughly enjoys his new outlook. Only a *wish* may restore the former alignment.

Also, the drink causes the imbiber to permanently to lose 4 points of constitution as he or she wretches and vomits incessantly for the rest of his days or until the curse is removed.

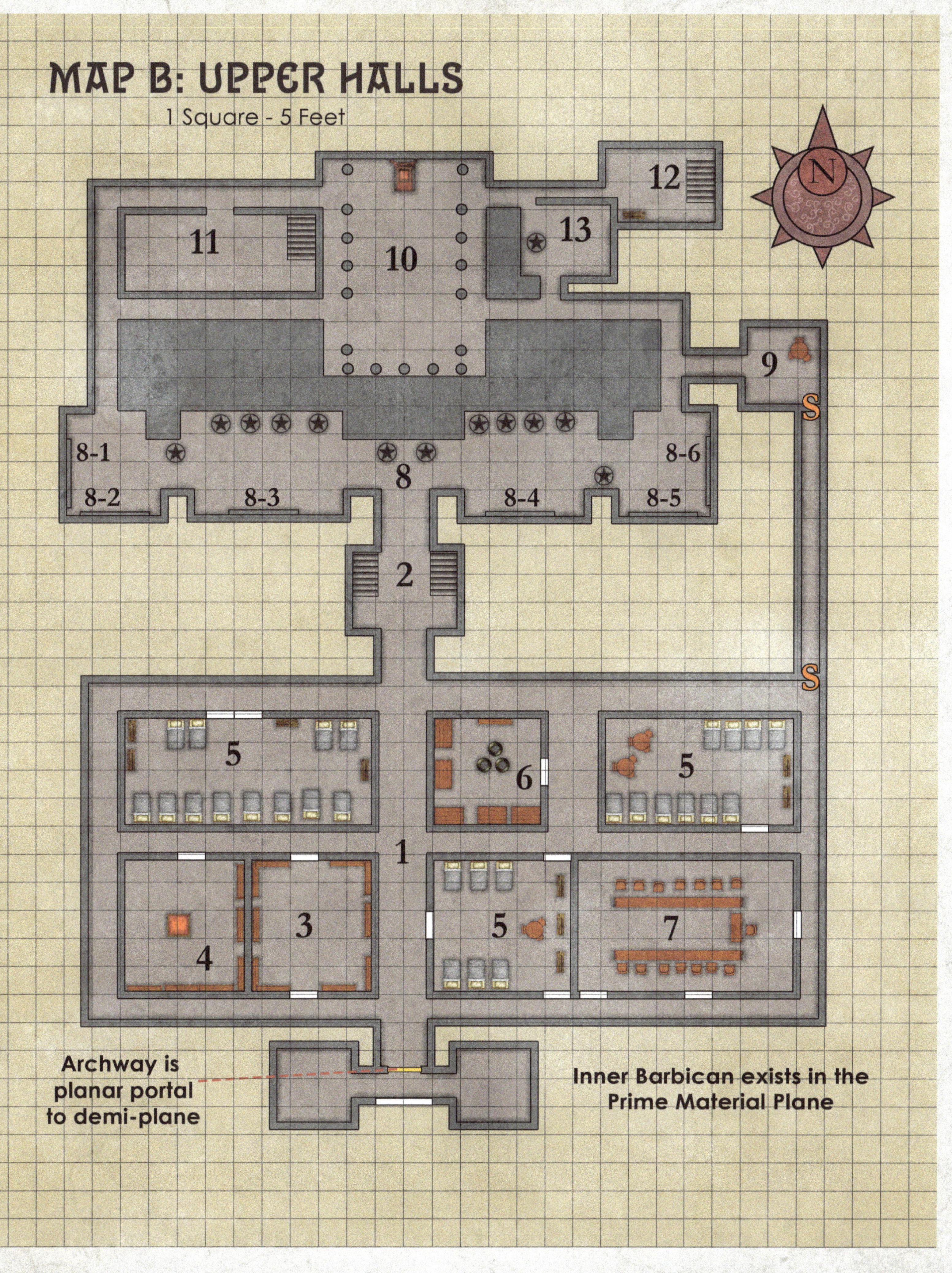

MAP B: UPPER HALLS
1 Square - 5 Feet
N
11
10
12
13
9
S
S
8-1
8-2
8-3
8
8-4
8-5
8-6
2
5
6
5
1
3
4
5
7
Archway is planar portal to demi-plane
Inner Barbican exists in the Prime Material Plane

S
Archway planar portal is directly behind secret door
7
3
10
S
6
8
9
7
N
1
MAP C: LOWER HALLS
1 Square - 5 Feet
2
4
5

**Oozespouter, Female Human Brother of the Ooze (Mnk4): HP** 13; **AC** 4[15]; **Atk** strike (1d8); **Move** 15; **Save** 12; **AL** N; **CL/XP** 6/400; **Special:** +1 save vs. charm, confusion and fear spells, +2 save vs. paralysis and poison, +2 weapon damage bonus, +2 save vs. paralysis and poison, +2 weapon damage bonus, 1-in-6 chance of being surprised, deadly strike (when attack roll is 5 higher than needed, 75% chance to be stunned for 2d6 rounds, 25% chance to kill enemy), deflect missiles (saving throw), litany of chaos (3/day, chant confuses enemies, save or stand confused for 1d4 rounds), ooze armor (+2 AC bonus, excretes from pores, similar to phlegm in color and consistency), purity of slime (1/day, summon ooze, 20% chance [5% chance per level]; roll 1d6: 1–2, grey ooze; 3–4, crystal ooze; 5–6, black pudding), summon lesser ooze demon (1/week, 8% chance [2% chance per level], serves for 1 hour), thieving skills, speak with animals.

**Thieving Skills:** Climb 88%, Tasks/Traps 30%, Hear 4 in 6, Hide 25%, Silent 35%, Locks 25%.

**Equipment:** simple robes, *potion of levitate*, 1d8 gems (1d4 x 100 gp).

*Description:* Oozespouter is a thick and squat woman. She has extremely short-cropped brown hair, and boils are everywhere on her skin. She wears a bright pink robe that is torn. She is prone to breaking down and bawling during combat.

*Background:* Oozespouter was stolen from an orphanage by Quagmire when she was a very young girl. Living the life of a virtual slave, she idolized Quagmire and emulated every aspect of him. She is also completely infatuated with Sludgebearer, who has been reluctantly showing her the ways of the monk.

*Motivation:* Oozespouter deeply desires to be accepted. She always tried to find this acceptance from Quagmire; later, she tried to find what she desires from Sludgebearer. Although Sludgebearer has taught her some of his skills, Oozespouter still yearns for guidance. Of the brotherhood, she is the most likely to help the characters.

Oozespouter surrenders to the characters if battle is hopeless for the brotherhood. She bows down and begs for mercy immediately. This act enrages the other members of the brotherhood and they attack her.

Once in a situation where Oozespouter is on speaking terms with the characters (as opposed to at the business end of a weapon), she attempts to escape at the earliest possible opportunity. If the characters make a bargain with her, however, she keeps the bargain. Oozespouter prizes her life and is highly motivated by evenhanded promises to spare her life in exchange for cooperation. Dark threats only encourage her to run during the next battle in which the characters participate.

*Tactics:* The characters likely catch the brotherhood offguard. The brotherhood is immediately hostile to the characters if they are in the company of the Cabal of the Beard since the brotherhood hates all dwarves for imprisoning their lord. If possible, the brotherhood attempts to learn what the characters are doing before attacking. The brotherhood has no idea what the key is, but makes many inquiries about it. If the brotherhood somehow learns that the key opens the vault, they make a grab for it and attempt a mad dash for the exit.

## The Silver Eyes

The Silver Eyes were originally a group of drow who came to the surface seeking their lot among the "weaker species." Running afoul of their patron demoness, they left the Under Realms in the service of a new patron — a duke of the hells. At this devil's behest, the Silver Eyes recently "replaced" one of their members with another Under Realms' outcast: an encephalon gorger. Although the devil rarely calls upon their service, he has sent many visions to them ordering the retrieval of the Faceless Lord's amulet.

The Silver Eyes are a methodical and calculating bunch of rogues. They do not attack unless confident that their plan will work. In other words, the Silver Eyes constantly monitor the situation with *clairvoyance* and other means of scrying before attacking.

The bone devil spy (see **Chapter Three**) is an advanced scout for the Silver Eyes. His report (or lack thereof) spurs the group into action. This group could be placed in either the "Siege of Orcus" or "Necromantic Dreams."

**Mandan Silvereyes, Female Drow (Ftr 4/Thf4): HP** 25; **AC** 4[15]; **Atk** *+1 warhammer* (1d4+2) or *javelin of lightning* (1d6) or javelin (1d6); **Move** 12; **Save** 8/9 (includes +2 save bonus and +1, ring); **AL** C; **CL/XP** 10/1400; **Special:** +2 on all saving throws, +2 save bonus vs. traps and magical devices, backstab (x2), darkvision (60ft), magic resistance (50%), multiple attacks (4) vs. creatures with 1 or fewer HD, read languages, spell-like abilities, surprise enemies (75% chance), thieving skills, vulnerability (–2 to-hit penalty in sunlight).

**Spell-like abilities:** at will—*darkness 15ft radius*, create lights (60ft range), outline targets with faint light (+1 to hit).

**Thieving Skills:** Climb 88%, Tasks/Traps 30%, Hear 4 in 6, Hide 40%, Silent 45%, Locks 25%.

**Equipment:** *+2 leather armor*, cloak, boots, *+1 warhammer*, 3 *javelins of lightning* (see sidebar), 4 javelins, *bag of holding*, *ring of protection +1*, *potion of extra healing*, *potion of invisibility*, bag with 285 gp, 3d4 gems of various value.

*Description:* Mandan Silvereyes is a gorgeous drow elf with flowing white hair and flashing silver eyes. She is as deadly as she is beautiful, however. She wears banded mail covered in carvings of drow figures performing unspeakable acts. Mandan carries a large, crude hammer, a boon from a battle with deep gnomes.

*Background:* Mandan Silvereyes began life as a scion of a powerful drow household. Yet like many drow scions, her house was destroyed before she could assassinate her way to power. She lays the blame for this event at the feet of the Queen of Spiders. Thus, she has no time for spiders. Finding other "orphans" of a similar mind, she led them to the surface and rules them through wit and will. Jurak threatens her position, however, because of guidance from the devil they serve.

*Motivation:* Greed, lust, and self-preservation motivate Mandan Silvereyes. She may change goals on a whim. She will, though, plan any confrontation thoroughly. She cares little about the other members of her group and sees them only as pawns to help her accomplish her goals.

### Unusual Weapon

#### Javelin of Lightning

This black and silver javelin crackles with electricity when thrown at a target. If the wielder makes a successful to-hit roll, the javelin turns into a lightning bolt that travels in a straight line toward the target. Any creature in the path (including the original target) takes 4d6 points of damage from the bolt unless they make a saving throw for half damage. If the attack misses, the lightning damage is expended harmlessly. The javelin can be used in this fashion once per day, although it can still be used as a normal javelin during this time.

**Epar Griz, Male Drow (Thf9): HP** 31; **AC** 7[12]; **Atk** *+1 short sword* (1d6+1) or *+1 dagger* (1d4+1) or light crossbow (1d4+1); **Move** 24 (*boots of speed*); **Save** 3 (includes +2 save bonus and +2, cloak); **AL** C; **CL/XP** 11/1700; **Special:** +2 on all saving throws, +2 save bonus vs. traps and magical devices, backstab (x4), darkvision (60ft), magic resistance (50%), read languages, spell-like abilities, surprise enemies (75% chance), thieving skills, vulnerability (–2 to-hit penalty in sunlight).

**Spell-like abilities:** at will—*darkness 15ft radius*, create lights (60ft range), outline targets with faint light (+1 to hit).

**Thieving Skills:** Climb 93%, Tasks/Traps 60%, Hear 5 in 6, Hide 80%, Silent 80%, Locks 65%.

**Equipment:** *cloak of protection +2*, *boots of speed*, *+1 short sword*, *+1 dagger*, light crossbow, 12 bolts, 3 *potions of frozen concoctions*, bag with 83 gp and 1d6 gems of various values.

*Description:* Epar Griz is boastful and arrogant. He wears a black scarf on his head and occasionally spits between a huge gap in his front teeth. Epar never sits still and has a tendency to talk rapidly (spraying spit all over whomever he is talking to). Epar Griz wears no armor because he is amazingly quick.

*Background:* Epar Griz tells whoever will listen that he is a bastard child of a high priestess. The truth is that his boasting is a veil for the fact that he is actually a drow of low birth. Also, despite his arrogance, he is actually a very good thief.

*Motivation:* Like Mandan, Epar Griz is motivated by coin. The adventure and constant danger he and his companions experience excites him. Epar is wary of the recent addition of the encephalon gorger and absolutely hates the worship of the devil — to whom he is only paying lip service for the time being.

**Jurak Grubber, Female Drow Priestess of Orcus (Clr8): HP** 39; **AC** 0[19]; **Atk** *+1 flail* (1d8+1); **Move** 12; **Save** 6 (includes +2 save bonus); **AL** C; **CL/XP** 10/1400; **Special:** +2 on all saving throws, +2 save vs. paralysis or poison, control undead, darkvision (60ft), magic resistance (50%), spell-like abilities, spells (2/2/2/2/2), surprise enemies (75% chance), vulnerability (–2 to-hit penalty in sunlight).

**Spell-like abilities:** at will—*darkness 15ft radius*, create lights (60ft range), outline targets with faint light (+1 to hit).

**Spells:** 1st—*cure light wounds, detect magic;* 2nd—*hold person, snake charm;* 3rd—*locate object, speak with dead;* 4th—*cure serious wounds, sticks to snakes;* 5th—*commune, finger of death.*

**Equipment:** *+1 plate mail, +1 shield, +1 flail,* scroll (*find traps, silence 15ft radius*), scroll (*cure disease*), scroll (*cure light wounds*).

*Description:* Jurak Grubber is an attractive drow who shaved off all her hair, leaving only a topknot. She frequently uses white makeup to create a skull visage on her face. Jurak communicates with the devil who sent them on the mission to retrieve the amulet from the characters; however, she receives her powers from her true master, Orcus. Although younger than the other drow, her fervor and devotion to Orcus gained her an ally in Sinad.

*Background:* Jurak, like Mandan, was a progeny of a noble drow house. Yet unlike Mandan, her house was not destroyed. Instead, Jurak willingly left to discover more of the Lord of Undead after learning of him from a visiting encephalon gorger dignitary. Jurak wants to lead the group back into the Under Realms, as she has megalomaniacal dreams of converting all drow to Orcus.

*Motivation:* Jurak is a megalomaniac; she believes that Orcus has made her nearly invincible. She views Mandan with disdain, but sees her as a tolerable nuisance until she gains enough of Orcus' favor to lead an army of undead to convert the drow populace. She is excited that the encephalon gorger joined them because it tilted the scales in the group in her favor over Mandan. She feels great distaste in working with the devil, but she plots to take the amulet for Orcus.

**Sinad, Male Drow (MU12):** HP 34; AC 6[13] or 2[17] (missile) and 4[15] (melee) from *shield* spell; **Atk** *staff of power* (2d6) or *+1 dagger* (1d4+1); **Move** 12; **Save** 3 (includes +2 save bonus); **AL** C; **CL/XP** 14/2600; **Special:** +2 on all saving throws, +2 save vs. spells, wands and staffs, darkvision (60ft), magic resistance (50%), spell-like abilities, spells (4/4/4/4/4/1), surprise enemies (75% chance), vulnerability (–2 to-hit penalty in sunlight).

**Spell-like abilities:** at will—*darkness 15ft radius,* create lights (60ft range), outline targets with faint light (+1 to hit).

**Spells:** 1st—*detect magic, magic missile, shield, sleep;* 2nd—*ESP, invisibility, phantasmal force, web;* 3rd—*clairvoyance, dispel magic, lightning bolt, slow;* 4th—*confusion,* dimension door, polymorph self, wizard eye; 5th—*animate dead, contact other plane, feeblemind, transmute rock to mud;* 6th—*disintegrate.*

**Equipment:** *bracers of defense AC 6[13], staff of power, +1 dagger, bag of holding, figurine of the onyx dog,* scroll (*monster summoning II*), scroll (*protection from normal missiles*), scroll (*fireball* [x2], *hold person, levitate*), scroll (*charm person, detect invisibility, suggestion*), *wand of magic missiles* (12 charges),

*Description:* Sinad is a morose drow who left the Under Realms to learn more of the surface world. He is quiet and rarely speaks. When he does speak, however, Mandan usually considers his words. Sinad is secretly in love with Jurak. He wears a long drow robe of bluish hue and has a large mane of white hair and piercing violet eyes.

*Background:* Sinad's parents ordered his death when he refused to yield his position as a high wizard to lead his family's estate. Eventually, he dealt with his parents by devastating the household and killing many of its servants. These acts made him an outcast, and Mandan eventually recruited him.

*Motivation:* Sinad is quiet and calculating, but he has the potential for great destruction (as his parents discovered). Sinad bears a deep affection for Jurak. Although he usually sides with her, his intellect does not allow him to let emotions rule his mind. He is curious about the encephalon gorger and sometimes engages it in hours of metaphysical discussion.

**Bleela, Encephalon Gorger:** HD 8; HP 59; AC 6[13]; **Atk** 2 claws (1d6+1 + mindfeed); **Move** 6; **Save** 8; **AL** C; **CL/XP** 9/1100; **Special:** haste (2/day, as spell), mindfeed (if 2 claws hit target, start to drain cerebral fluid in next round, 1d6 damage per round), regenerate (3hp/round), resist cold (50% damage). (***The Tome of Horrors Complete*** 234)

*Description:* Bleela is a typical encephalon gorger. She (it refers to itself as she) wears long purple and pink robes, a square hat, and many jewels and gold trinkets.

*Background:* Bleela was ordered to serve a visiting priest of Orcus as part of an evil pact between the church of Orcus and the encephalon gorgers. The priest in turn gave Bleela's service to Jurak (immediately before Jurak murdered the priest). Bleela then disposed of the previous party member, whom Jurak did not like. She is very much a cold and calculating killer.

*Motivation:* Bleela thinks not of herself. She has devoted herself in undertaking the boon to the servants of Orcus until such time that the service is at an end. At that time, Bleela simply feeds on the minds of her companions and returns to her former life.

## Imbo the Undying

Born to a whore — this is how Imbo began life in the cruel world. Reminded of his parentage and the limitless possibilities of his father, the young dwarf was beaten and brutalized throughout his childhood. Eventually running away from his broken home, Imbo was captured by a group of barbarian raiders.

Unaware of Imbo's past, the barbarians treated Imbo the same as they treated all of their children — that is, poorly. The barbarians trained Imbo to track, to hunt, and to wield a warhammer. Imbo learned his lessons well, but was ever the outsider, not being human born.

In adolescence, Imbo began to covet wealth. When booty was available, Imbo frequently held back a shiny object or item. Later, he began to steal items. Although there were whispers and a few open accusations, nothing was done to the dwarf. Late one night, Imbo tried to steal the warband leader's golden horn. The chieftain caught Imbo in this treacherous act, and Imbo slew his foster father in a fit of rage. He then fled into the night.

Many years later, Imbo was an accomplished thief. He found his way into a village of elves. After an elf insulted his parentage (although the elf had no idea of the truth of it), Imbo went on a bloody spree. Within hours, the entire village was either dead or had fled into the wilderness.

The final victim for Imbo's cruelty was an ancient and withered elf, but she did not beg for mercy. Before dying, she told Imbo, "For the blackness of your heart and the sins you commit, you shall be ever reminded and know no rest."

Imbo learned later the actual effect of the curse: He could not die. He could be subdued, disintegrated, or even, on one occasion, consumed; however, his life would always, eventually come back. His anger at this prospect grew greater as the years wore on.

Now fully consumed by hatred, Imbo has become wrath incarnate. Thoroughly evil, Imbo does not hesitate to commit the foulest acts that his perverse mind can concoct. Menacing and brooding, Imbo does not hesitate to rain his ever-burning hatred upon those around him to occupy the emptiness in his soul that the fates have spun for him.

Particularly wealthy and evil individuals frequently hire Imbo as a mercenary. An astute warrior, a remarkable thief, and an evil force unto himself, Imbo is without remorse, without fear, and he brings carnage wherever he roams.

**Imbo the Undying, Male Dwarf (Ftr9/Thf5):** HP 70; AC 5[14]; **Atk** *+2 thrown warhammer that returns to the hand* (1d4+8) or *+1 battleaxe* (1d8+7); **Move** 9; **Save** 6/11; **AL** C; **CL/XP** 15/2900; **Special:** +2 save bonus vs. traps and magical devices, +4 save vs. magic, automatic resurrection (body reforms 24 hours after death), backstab (x3), darkvision (60ft), multiple attacks (9) vs. creatures with 1 or fewer HD, read languages, thieving skills.

**Thieving Skills:** Climb 89%, Tasks/Traps 45%, Hear 4 in 6, Hide 35%, Silent 45%, Locks 35%.

**Equipment:** *+2 leather armor, gauntlets of ogre power, +2 thrown warhammer that returns to the hand, +1 battleaxe, ring of invisibility.*

## Raob and Sleeara

Another set of NPCs could be Raob and Sleeara (see **Chapter One**). Placing these two with a number of Raob's sergeants would be an easy way for you to deal with characters needing to eliminate Raob and his army completely if they leave the Citadel.

Basically, any dead guards or any sign of disturbance shows Sleeara that someone entered the Citadel. She already knows that the army has been digging directly into the granite and not finding any artifacts, bodies, or even rooms. She already suspects something. With her knowledge of arcana, the Devil's Finger, and dwarven magic, she and Raob could travel back in time and into the Citadel in either the "Siege of Orcus" or "Necromantic Dreams."

**Lord Raob Blackenheart, Male Human Warrior (Ftr12):** HP 70; AC 1[18]; **Atk** *+2 heavy flail* (1d8+8); **Move** 12; **Save** 4; **AL** C; **CL/XP** 12/2000; **Special:** multiple attacks (12) vs. creatures with 1 or fewer HD.

**Equipment:** *+2 plate mail,* helm, *+2 heavy flail, gauntlets of ogre power.*

**Sleeara, Female Human Necromancer (MU10):** HP 34; AC 8[11] or 2[17] (missile) and 4[15] (melee) from *shield* spell; **Atk** *staff of power* (2d6) or *+1 dagger* (1d4+1); **Move** 12; **Save** 6 (+1, ring); **AL** C; **CL/XP** 11/1700; **Special:** +2 save vs. spells, wands and staffs, spells (4/4/3/2/2).

**Spells:** 1st—*charm person* (x2), *magic missile, shield;* 2nd—*detect good, ESP, invisibility, phantasmal force;* 3rd—*hold person, lightning bolt, suggestion;* 4th—*polymorph other, wall of ice;* 5th—*animate dead* (x2).

**Equipment:** *robe of wizardry, staff of power, +1 dagger, ring of protection +1,* pockets full of spell components.

**Note:** Sleeara hides her spellbook in her room in the Fest Haus.

**Sergeants, Male or Female Humans (Ftr6) (8 or as needed):**
**HD** 6; **HP** 47, 45, 43, 41x2, 39, 37, 34; **AC** 5[14]; **Atk** bastard sword
(1d8) or longbow x2 (1d6); **Move** 12; **Save** 9; **AL** C; **CL/XP** 6/400;
**Special:** multiple attacks (5) vs. creatures with 1 or fewer HD. (see
**Encounter I-B**)
**Equipment:** black chainmail, red cape, bastard sword, longbow, 30
arrows, 1d4 gems (1d10x10 gp).

# DWURSCHMIEDE: THE CITADEL

The following areas of the Citadel are briefly described. They are depicted on
**Map B: Citadel Upper Level** and **Map C: Citadel Lower Level**. The appropriate
sets of encounters are left for you to insert, depending on which era the characters
are currently investigating (either the "Siege of Orcus" or "Necromantic Dreams").
This is an excellent opportunity to challenge fully but not overwhelm the characters
by scaling the encounters up or down where appropriate.

## AREA B-1: THE GRAND HALL

A long hallway lies before the characters. Colorful banners hang from a 20-foot-
high ceiling and depict horns, a helm, an axe, and similar symbols. As well, a large
red and black banner proclaims these halls as the abode of Clan Flammeaxte. The
granite has changed from the rough grayish rock as it appears outside on the surface
of the Devil's Finger. Here, the granite is a polished red. Arches carved in the ceiling
proclaim in an ancient Dwarven dialect, "Welcome Friend!" and "Death to Fiend!"
Small, five-foot-wide-by-five-foot-tall hallways lead off on both sides.

## AREA B-2: THE STAIRS

Hanging from a 20-foot-high ceiling is an elaborate black, wrought-iron
candelabra. On opposite walls, two sets of polished stairs lead down. To the north,
the corridor splits left and right. Lining the walls to the north are polished skulls of
orcs, elves, and other humanoids. Mixed among them are strange black skills with
spiraling horns and large fanged teeth.

The candelabra is raised and lowered by a chain in the northwest corner. A stone
bench is in the corner for the guards. A dwarf-hair blanket is underneath the bench.
The dwarves of the Citadel in times of shame cut off their beards, and their wives
and loved ones routinely take the hair and make it into something useful as a symbol
of redemption.

The stairs here are trapped. In each staircase is a random stair an inch or two
shorter than the rest and requires each character to make a saving throw or trip
and take 1d6 points of damage. This rudimentary trap is to trip invaders who are
unfamiliar with the stairs. The characters will likely encounter someone in this
heavily trafficked area; roll for the possibility of a random encounter in either time
period.

## AREA B-3: WORKSHOP

Wooden benches and tables line the perimeter of this room. A large brazier sits
in the center. On the wall are wooden pegs with aprons hanging from them. Runes
written along the ceiling at odd intervals proclaim the greatness of Dwurfater and
ask for his blessing in the crafting below.

## AREA B-4: STORAGE

This room has numerous stone shelves full of metal boxes and foodstuffs. The
dwarves use this room to store food and basic supplies (bandages, empty flasks,
dried meats, and so forth). In a corner is a broken wooden spoon where a particularly
greedy dwarf was eating the stores. Bundles of twine are also lying about. Other
than these ordinary items, there is nothing special about these rooms.

## AREA B-5: BARRACKS

Rows of triple bunk beds line this room; the beds are made of stained wood.
Weapons and armor are ready for use in racks lining the wall. A few footlockers are
set near the beds. Several piles of stones — chits from gambling games played by
the dwarves — are in the corner of one of the barracks. A small kobold drum made
of human skin and bone that has "Gog" written on it is in another.

## AREA B-6: KITCHEN

Various iron pots hang from the low ceiling of this room. A shelf carved in the
wall has numerous tins for dwarven spices, and painted on the tins are such names
as "shale oil," "mountain mint," and "sprig of toadstool." The spice rack has a
recipe for Kobold Kidney Pie carved into it. Large black pots sit on stoves cut into
the floor. Small, three-inch-wide chimneys carry the smoke from the stoves into the
Finger. The entire area is very cramped and crowded.

## AREA B-7: MESS HALL

Long wooden tables and chairs form a square in this room. Shields with dwarven
heraldry are set on the walls. A large chair — the only chair in the room — sits at
one end of the square. Numerous brass steins hang on one wall, and a forgotten
brass tapper lies underneath a bench. At each place on the tables are placed a small
wooden spoon, a sharp knife, and a wooden plate.

## AREA B-8: HALL OF HEROES

Numerous carvings and statues line the length of this hall from west to east. All
the statues depict menacing, snarling dwarves with large axes. The carvings show
the Citadel's history.

The first carving depicts a mountain and a great cube falling from the sky. The
mountain breaks apart in the next pane, with a dwarf in the corner covering his head
with an arm. The third pane shows the Devil's Finger where the mountain once
stood with the cube on its top.

The second carving shows dwarves climbing to the top of the Citadel. The
second pane shows an upside-down crescent with spikes protruding from it in
all directions within the cube and the dwarves kneeling and worshipping it. Very
observant individuals notice tiny eyes with flecks of ruby all over the stone carving.
The shards are worthless. The third pane shows a great dwarf god looking over a
cloud high above the Citadel with a look of disbelief on his face.

The third carving shows the great dwarf god pointing at his worshippers. The
next pane shows row after row of dwarven smiths hammering on a gigantic anvil.
The final pane displays a circle of dwarves surrounding the anvil beneath the
Devil's Finger.

The fourth carving depicts the anvil sitting atop the cube. A rising moon in the
distance is smeared with a brown paint that looks like dried blood. The next pane
shows a column of swirling liquid with many eyes. In the final pane, the dwarf god
smiles above the crescent. Spikes are on top of the anvil, which sits on top of the
cube, which rests on top of the swirling column.

The fifth carving shows the dwarf god looking down from a cloud high above the
Devil's Finger, pointing at the cube. The next two panes show construction of the
Citadel's towers and barbican.

The sixth carving is visible in "Necromantic Dreams" but not in the "Siege of
Orcus." It shows demons invading the halls of the Citadel. If the characters assisted
the dwarves in defeating the demons, it shows the faces and bodies of the characters
and describes in two panes the events that transpired earlier. Alternately, it could
show the characters decimating the dwarves or the dwarves driving them back and
defeating them.

## AREA B-9: GUARD ROOM

This side guard room is the station area for the lord of the Citadel's personal
guards. The guards use the secret passage only in emergencies to escape or to flank
any assault in the stair area. The room has a small round table with chairs. The table
has many notches, the result of the guards keeping score while playing dice or other
games. A cracked ivory pipe is on the table.

## AREA B-10: GREAT HALL

This is the grand reception hall of the Citadel's lord. Great columns are carved
from the same stone as the ceiling and the floor. These columns are ornately
decorated with dwarven runes that list the many dwarves who died creating the
Citadel. On the far end is a great throne on a dais that rises five feet above the floor.
Both throne and dais are carved directly out of the granite. The throne is in the shape
of an anvil with a depression in it for the lord of the Citadel to sit. The ceiling of the
room is 40 feet high. This room is directly beneath the vault.

## AREA B-11: GUEST QUARTERS

This is one of the most elaborately furnished rooms in the Citadel. It has an
unusual bed of elaborate craftsmanship. The wooden bed is canopied and can be
adjusted in length or width to fit any creature from three to seven feet tall. A large
painting on one wall depicts dwarves fighting elves. The scene in the painting,
however, changes as one moves by it. From one angle, it shows the battle; from
another angle, it shows the elves and dwarves embracing as brothers. It is magical
and was a gift from an elf diplomat. (See the sidebar for more information on the
*painting of enlightenment*.)

The room also contains chairs, a dressing table, and a rack for weapons and
armor. A large ogre skin rug lies on the floor. The ogre's skull is on display near the
stairs (**Area B-2**).

The lord of the Citadel during the "Siege of Orcus" is King Galm. His spartan lifestyle removed all frivolity from the room. There is a simple, hard bed, a rack for his greataxe, and a stand for his elaborate armor. A footstool hidden underneath the bed has an elf's face on it. Galm said that he would use the stool to talk eye-to-eye with elves, but demanded that he be allowed to step on an elf's face to do so.

---

### Lesser Miscellaneous Magical Item

#### Painting of Enlightenment

A *painting of enlightenment* is a magical work of art. The scene depicted on the painting appears to move, its motion dependent upon the viewer's position in relation to the painting. If the viewer shuffles left to right, the particular scene is viewed in chronological sequence. If, however, the viewer moves right to left when beholding the painting, the scene plays out in reverse — horses appear to run backward, the sun sets in the east, and so on. A *painting of enlightenment* may depict any event, real or imagined, that the artist desires, though the detail of the scenes is restricted by the physical size of the canvas.

On the day the characters view the Citadel's *painting of enlightenment*, it shows a struggle between dwarves and elves. As the characters move through time, the painting shows other scenes. In the catacombs, the painting is about the hanging of a dwarf traitor, and it might change to show demons overcoming and killing Lord Galm. In "Necromantic Dreams," the painting depicts the coming of the priest and his army, the courage of the last dwarves defending the Citadel, and the death of the priest. A *painting of enlightenment* could thus be used in any campaign to foreshadow events or relate histories.

---

## Area B-13: Reception Area

A map of the surrounding countryside is inlaid on the floor in this room. The only furniture is a large throne for the Citadel's lord, who comes here in order to make plans to repel sieges. A large ruby is set in the center of the map. Anyone saying "map" in an ancient dwarven dialect activates an illusion showing the Devil's Finger and the surrounding countryside. This is the only means by which the dwarves kept track of the immediate outside world. Although traveling to the outside world was forbidden, there were times when the dwarves made small excursions. The ruby can be removed with a successful Delicate Tasks check. A failed check destroys the stone. The ruby does not function if removed and is worth 5,000 gp.

## Area C-1: Stairs Below

This area is identical to the stairs on the upper level (**Area B-2**). This stair, however, had a trap that was triggered with the arrival of the demons in the "Siege of Orcus." The trap released large boulders and rubble to block the south passageway.

## Area C-2: Forge

This large area is the Citadel's central smithing facility. Numerous forges, bellows, and elaborate chimneys line the walls. The chimneys are made of metal and take the heat and smoke off at angles; they enter the walls and funnel the smoke and fires to the side of the Citadel. The very-narrow chimneys cannot be traversed by any non-magical means. In the center of the room are a number of anvils that form a circle around a small statue of Dwurfater that shows the god with a sour expression on his face, as if he is never satisfied with the smiths.

## Area C-3: Kinst's Chambers

This is the bedchambers of Kinst, the traitor. Kinst has very gaudy taste for a dwarf. A number of chalk drawings on the wall show the Devil's Finger from various angles. Each drawing is signed with a gigantic Dwarven "K." The drawings emphasize the vault, making it appear larger than it is in reality. Kinst's bed is a simple cot, but he has an elaborately carved dresser and the only mirror in the entire Citadel.

The wall-mounted mirror is magical and allows Kinst to communicate with others outside the Citadel. The mirror functions exactly like a *crystal ball*. Orcus plotted with Kinst concerning the Citadel's demise through this mirror. If removed from the wall, the mirror loses its magical properties.

## Area C-4: Armory

Rack after rack of weapons and armor stand ready to be used against any aggressors who attack the Citadel. You must decide what the characters find here. A few of the weapons are magical, but most of those weapons are already in the possession of the dwarves encountered in the "Siege of Orcus" due to the preparations for the demon invasion.

## Area C-5: Storage

This massive storage area holds food and drinking water. A font in the middle of the room magically provides spring water; the water is drinkable in either dimension. The foodstuffs are either pungent dwarven cheeses, hearty ales, disgusting brandy, hard breads, and dried meats in the "Siege of Orcus," or dust on empty shelves in "Necromantic Dreams."

## Area C-6: Temple of Dwurfater

This room has a high ceiling with columns identical to the Great Hall (**Area C-11**). At the far end is an altar upon which rests a large statue of Dwurfater readying a great blow with his hammer on a large anvil. Behind Dwurfater is a secret door; a hammer can be obtained from **Area C-4**. The hammer in Dwurfater's hand is part of the stone block from which the statue was carved. Breaking the hammer from the statue and using it to hit the anvil does nothing. The anvil shows many depressions from a hammer striking it. Below the anvil is an inscription in an ancient dialect of Dwarven that reads: "With a Dwarven Blow, I Protect My Children."

This is the only way to open the magical door, as it was created by arcane dwarven magics.

## Area C-7: Priest Quarters

This is the quarters of the priests attending to Usis, the high priest of Dwurfater. This room has a number of beds and tables. Many holy symbols are carved into the ceiling, arranged in a circle and depicting the dwarven pantheon with Dwurfater's anvil large in the center.

## Area C-8: Usis' Quarters

Usis, high priest of Dwurfater, made his home here. During the "Siege of Orcus," he fell very ill and is comatose with priests attending him. This was the work of Kinst. The room has a simple cot, a small anvil shrine to Dwurfater, and an unlocked chest full of vestments and robes.

## Area C-9: Burial Preparation and Masonry

Most dwarves are burned in the great forges when they die. For the kings, their tenure as guardians remains in the afterlife. The priests use this room to prepare these bodies after death for burial in the catacombs below. The dwarves are not experts in mummification, but they do use oils and spices to prepare the body; a long stone slab is used for this purpose. Funerary oils and spices that smell very caustic are on a shelf.

The other part of the room is a storage area for mining tools (picks, shovels, and carts). These are sacramental tools used by the new dwarven king to bury the recently deceased lord. The mining tools are always caked with stone dust, for cleaning them is sacrilege, and they are usually lying about haphazardly.

## Area C-10: Lower Archway

Hidden behind the statue of Dwurfater (**Area C-6**) is the lower archway, which is identical to the upper archway. This lower archway is accessible only with the rune belonging to the dwarven king, without which anyone entering the archway is lost through time. It is visible only from the stairwell side. Looking back through the archway, the characters see most of the temple collapsed due to the temporal anchors protecting the archway. Entering the archway from the catacomb side sends the characters into "Necromantic Dreams."

The stairwell is a gigantic spiral staircase. The center is open, and the end of the stairs is 75 feet below.

The characters enter the Citadel's demiplane through the upper archway. At the same time, the characters travel back 3,000 years and arrive during a siege by the minions of Orcus. A traitor to the dwarves is about to open a *gate*. Orcus wants to overrun the dwarves and take the Faceless Lord's amulet for himself and add to his own power.

The specific encounters described herein pertain to a *gate* that opens moments after the characters arrive. Orcus conspired with a cowardly dwarf priest named Kinst. With the dwarf's assistance, Orcus pierced the Citadel's magical wards to open the *gate*.

Orcus provided Kinst with the means to create an evil totem that activates the *gate*. The only way to destroy the *gate* is to destroy the totem. In other words, the *gate* functions as per the spell of the same name, except it is permanent and cannot be dispelled but for destroying the totem. This may be difficult for the characters to discern without speaking to Kinst or healing High Priest Usis.

The characters may also befriend the dwarves, which is most likely through the gregarious and charismatic King Galm. Galm is as frightened as any dwarf at first seeing the strange party (unless the party is all dwarves), but he accepts any reasonable explanation if the party is willing to address the current situation. Dwarves are watchful that an invasion is about to occur. The characters must talk quickly to convince the dwarves that they are friends and not foes, as described in **Encounter III-A**.

The demons do not see the party as an ally except in the most unlikely of circumstances. They are intent upon finding the key and taking it as soon as possible. The only avenue for the demons to escape is through the *gate*, and they cannot *gate* in additional reinforcements. Please note that a Lawful party can indeed summon monsters to its aid, as the magical energies that protect the Citadel allow such magics for the Citadel's defense. The prime goal is for the party to gain access to the catacombs where the key is kept.

If the characters have an easy time dealing with the demons, additional NPC parties from **Chapter Two** can enter the fray. In particular, Raob and Sleeara and/or Imbo the Undying are recommended.

The accompanying sidebar contains a recommended timeline of events. This timeline takes the encounters out of the static and into the dynamic. Also, the timeline assumes no character intervention. Moving the monsters and NPCs makes the battle more realistic; in addition, the intensity of the encounters increases as the demons rampage through the Citadel.

## INTRODUCTORY CHARACTERISTICS

**Wandering Monsters:** The entire Citadel is about to break out into chaos when the characters arrive. They might find the demons attempting to locate the lower archway, though they will more likely run into dwarves bent on routing the demons from their stronghold. Roll 1d20 every 10 minutes.

| 1d20 | Encounter |
| --- | --- |
| 1 | King Galm from **Encounter III-A** |
| 2–4 | 2d6 dwarves |
| 5 | The devil spy from **Encounter III-D** |
| 6–7 | 1d6+2 dretches |
| 8 | The 2 succubi and the dwarven smiths from **Encounter III-C** |
| 9 | A vrock fighting 1d6 dwarves |
| 10 | An NPC party (see **Chapter Two**) |
| 11–20 | No Encounter |

**Dretch Demons (1d6+2):** HD 4; AC 2[17]; Atk 2 claws (1d4), bite (1d6); **Move** 9; **Save** 13; **AL** C; **CL/XP** 6/400; **Special:** spell-like abilities. (*Monstrosities* 92)
**Spell-like abilities:** 1/day—*darkness 15ft radius*, stinking cloud (20ft radius, save or nauseated for 1d4+1 rounds), summon 1d4 giant rats.
**Dwarf Guards, Male or Female Dwarves (Ftr3):** HD 3; AC 4[15]; **Atk** warhammer (1d4); **Move** 9; **Save** 12; **AL** L; **CL/XP** 3/60; **Special:** +4 save vs. magic, darkvision (60ft), multiple attacks (3) vs. creatures with 1 or fewer HD. (*Monstrosities* 149)
**Equipment:** chainmail, shield, warhammer.
**Vrock Demon:** HD 8; AC 0[19]; **Atk** beak (1d6), 2 foreclaws (1d8), 2 rear claws (1d6); **Move** 12 (fly 18); **Save** 8; **AL** C; **CL/XP** 11/1700; **Special:** immune to fire, magic resistance (50%), spell-like abilities, summon demon (10% chance, vrock). (*Monstrosities* 105)
**Spell-like abilities:** at will—*darkness 15ft radius*.
**Shielding:** As previously described, using *teleport* or other forms of magic to exit the Citadel is impossible.
**Detections:** Characters detect strong evil in all rooms south of the stairwell on the lower level due to the presence of the *gate* and the demons.
**Standard Features:** Unless otherwise noted, all doors are on a central pivot and made of stone. The floor, walls, and ceiling are seamless. The rock is polished smooth and has a mirror-like quality; also, every noise echoes throughout the stone structure. Both of these qualities of the Citadel's environment make sneaking about or hiding very difficult (–20% Move Silently penalty). On the other hand, the echo effect makes it easier for a party to hear what is ahead and around the bend. As well, each room is as tall as wide, except where otherwise noted. Thus, a majority of hallways in the Citadel are only five feet tall. In these cramped areas, a character suffers a –2 penalty to attacks and saving throws. The entire Citadel is lit with heavily smoking torches that burn the characters' eyes in crowded areas.
**Maps Used:** Map B: The Citadel — The Upper Halls; Map C: The Citadel — The Lower Halls.

| Time (Minutes) | Event |
|---|---|
| Two days before the characters arrive | High Priest Usis has a vision of demons invading the Citadel. |
| One day before the characters arrive | Kinst poisons Usis. |
| 00:00 | The characters arrive. Kinst murders two dwarves in the armory. |
| + 10:00 | Kinst opens the gate. Immediately, dretches arrive and begin wandering the Citadel. Various demons enter and begin attacking the dwarves on all levels. |
| + 12:00 | King Galm becomes aware of the invasion. The order is given to seal the southern halls on Level Two. King Galm desires to fight, but his advisors restrain him for fear that the *portal rune* to the catacombs might fall into the enemy's hands. |
| + 13:00 | Gleegog and Tarashix (**Encounter III-E**) arrive to secure the gate. |
| + 15:00 | The southern rubble trap is sprung (**Encounter III-B**). |
| + 20:00 | The bone devil (**Encounter III-E**) arrives and stealthily evades the demons guarding the gate. The bone devil makes its way to Kinst's chambers. |
| + 24:00 | Kainhis, leader of the demonic forces, arrives and heads toward **Encounter III-B**. |
| + 27:00 | Two succubi arrive to take control of the dwarves in **Encounter III-C**. |
| + 38:00 | Kainhis finishes devouring the dwarves at **Encounter III-B** and heads upstairs. |
| + 44:00 | The succubi take their dwarven "friends" and slay all of the healers in the northern halls on Level Two. They are assisted by demon reinforcements. |
| + 48:00 | Kainhis and other demons assault the Main Hall |
| + 61:00 | Kainhis kills Galm in his chambers. Demons cover her retreat to Level Two. |
| + 70:00 | The bone devil, realizing the battle is lost, makes its way back to the gate and leaves. |
| + 72:00 | All demons but Kainhis attack the remaining dwarves. Kinst begins to inscribe the *portal rune* onto himself. |
| + 80:00 | Kainhis enters the catacombs. All is lost. |

## DEFENDERS OF THE CITADEL AND LORD GALM

There are 140 dwarves in the complex. They are guards, priests, cooks, lords, and so forth. The adventure assumes that the party attempts to work with the dwarves, though you decide when and where these dwarves are encountered throughout the complex. Many of them might be sleeping, some might be on guard at the stairwell, others could be cooking, or the majority might be outside defending the battlements. By deciding where to place the dwarves, you can control the difficulty of this level.

On the other hand, if you anticipate that your party is likely to fight it out, most of the dwarves are stout 3rd-level fighters.

King Galm is in the reception area (**Area B-14**) working with his advisors. Ever since Usis' prophecy and seemingly related illness, Galm is preparing for the worst. The Citadel has not suffered a breach in almost 300 years, and one is not about to occur during his watch.

The characters will likely encounter King Galm very quickly. If they convince the dwarves in **Encounter III-A** that they are "friends" and not "foes," the dwarves immediately take the characters to Galm. He is loud, boisterous, and rude. He is a kind dwarf at heart, though, and is the first to believe the characters if they tell the truth of how they arrived at the Citadel. During this conversation, a guard rushes into the room warning of demons below. Galm wants to take care of this evil personally. Yet he is restrained. One of Galm's advisors — or perhaps Galm himself — recommends that the "purportedly good" characters remove the threat while the dwarves attempt to protect Galm and contain the demons that gained access to Level One. If the characters are amenable, this solidifies an alliance with the dwarves and is very likely to lead to Galm giving them the necessary *portal rune* to enter the catacombs (**Chapter Four**). If the characters bluntly refuse, Galm goes into a tirade and attempts to seize them. Galm is not afraid of any foe.

### LOCATION OF DWARVES

A typical distribution of the dwarves when the characters arrive is as follows:

| Location | Occupants |
|---|---|
| Upper Stairs | 6 dwarves — guards |
| Workshop | 5 dwarves — relentlessly crafting |
| Barracks | 20 dwarves — exhausted from battle and near comatose |
| Guard Room | 6 dwarves — guards |
| Great Hall | 4 dwarves — guards |
| Reception Area | King Galm and 8 dwarves |
| Lower Stairs | **Encounter III-B** |
| Forge | **Encounter III-C** |
| Kinst's Chambers | **Encounter III-D** |
| Armory | **Encounter III-E** |
| Temple | 2 priests and 10 dwarves |
| Usis' Chambers | Usis and 4 priests |

The comatose Usis is in his quarters, attended by 4 priests (with similar statistics as Alejan in **Encounter III-B**). Poisoned by Kinst (**Encounter III-D**), Usis is near death. The priests have been able to sustain him, but could use the characters help in healing Kinst fully. If they help (by casting *restoration*, *limited wish*, or a similar spell), he implicates Kinst and demands justice. Usis has received visions in his comatose state from Dwurfater and knows of his folly in trusting Kinst. If the characters are successful, the dwarves reward them with a *+2 warhammer* (*+4 vs. demons*) as a boon from the faithful of Dwurfater (this is Usis' personal weapon). Also, Usis may use the rune on the back of Galm's neck and tattoo the appropriate rune for the characters to move on to the catacombs.

**King Galm, Dwarf King, Male Dwarf (Ftr11):** HP 68; AC 2[17]; Atk *+2 battleaxe* (1d8+2); Move 9; Save 4; AL L; CL/XP 11/1700; **Special:** +4 save vs. magic, darkvision (60ft), multiple attacks (11) vs. creatures with 1 or fewer HD. (***Monstrosities*** 149)
**Equipment:** *+1 plate mail*, *+2 battleaxe*, crown (simple band of gold with 3 large rubies worth 2,000 gp).
**Dwarf Guards, Male or Female Dwarves (Ftr3):** HD 3; AC 4[15]; Atk warhammer (1d4) or shortbow x2 (1d6); Move 9; Save 12; AL L; CL/XP 3/60; **Special:** +4 save vs. magic, darkvision (60ft), multiple attacks (3) vs. creatures with 1 or fewer HD. (***Monstrosities*** 149)
**Equipment:** chainmail, shield, warhammer, shortbow, 35 arrows, 2d4 gems (1d10 gp each).
*Personality:* King Galm is very suspicious of any outsiders, but he may view them as a gift of Dwurfater to help the Citadel in its time of greatest need. See **Chapter Two** and above for more information on King Galm's motivations and personality. Galm has the only copy of the necessary *portal rune* that leads to the catacombs.

# Encounter III-A: Friend or Foe?
## (Area B-1)

As the characters enter the room through the archway on top of the Devil's Finger, they are immediately confronted with 15 dwarves led by Nukion, who is ordered to destroy any demon that enters the upper archway. One of the few dwarves allowed to leave the Dwurschmiede demiplane as a spy in the outside world, Nukion is very suspicious but recognizes the characters as being something other than a demon. Nukion is also the only dwarf who speaks Common. The others can understand Dwarven, but speak an ancient dialect.

The characters must talk their way out of a direct confrontation. If successful in calming down the frightened and potentially angry dwarves, the characters are immediately escorted to King Galm. Along the way, Nukion is likely to tell them proudly some of the history of Clan Flammeaxte.

If shown the *portal rune* the characters used to gain access to the Citadel, some of the dwarves might believe that they are celestials sent by Dwurfater to rout the demons. Whether the characters make this belief plausible is to be decided in the events and encounters to come.

**Nukion, Dwarf Commander, Male Dwarf (Ftr7):** HP 51; AC 4[15]; **Atk** +1 longsword (1d8+1); **Move** 9; **Save** 8; **AL** L; **CL/XP** 7/600; **Special:** +4 save vs. magic, darkvision (60ft), multiple attacks (7) vs. creatures with 1 or fewer HD. (***Monstrosities*** 149)
**Equipment:** chainmail, shield, *+1 longsword*, shortbow, 30 arrows, 2 *potions of healing*.
**Dwarf Guards, Male or Female Dwarves (Ftr3) (15):** HD 3; HP 22, 21x3, 20, 19, 18x5, 17, 16, 15x2; AC 4[15]; **Atk** warhammer (1d4); **Move** 9; **Save** 12; **AL** L; **CL/XP** 3/60; **Special:** +4 save vs. magic, darkvision (60ft), multiple attacks (3) vs. creatures with 1 or fewer HD. (***Monstrosities*** 149)
**Equipment:** chainmail, shield, warhammer.

# Encounter III-B: The Barricade
## (Area C-1)

Piles of bricks cover the south exit. Twelve dwarves stand with polearms before them pointing at the south pile. A small dwarf woman in a simple white robe grimaces, tears running down her cheek.

From beyond the south pile comes a muffled scream. Suddenly, the pile shifts and bricks clink together as they are pushed away from the top. Something horrifically foul, smelling of a combination of greasy manure and rotted flesh, is on the other side. The dwarves menacingly grit their teeth. "Stand fast, fellas," one utters.

At the top of the pile, a hole opens and a gigantic head pops through. With wild yellow eyes, bruise-purple skin, and a gigantic maw, the demon bellows a single word. The dwarves fall aside and break, fleeing in terror, and many fall to the ground in physical pain. The small priestess collapses under the assault, and the demon cackles with delight as it continues to break through the rubble.

The above description should be used if the characters are surprised (likely) by the demon. Although they might prepare themselves, the arrival of a demon combatant can shake any stout soul, causing hesitation.

The dwarves gathered here to make a stand against the newly arrived demons. By triggering a trap, the dwarves barricaded themselves behind a mass of bricks. The **hezrou** uses its *fear* ability to send the dwarves fleeing into the tunnels. The spell paralyzes the priestess Alejan. Not a warrior, Alejan is shocked by recent events and the arrival of the demon.

Faced with the scattered guards, the characters must now defend the Citadel or quickly move through the northern passage and attempt to find the lower archway.

Digging through the northern barrier requires 2d6 rounds of hard work.

**Alejan, Female Dwarf Cabal of the Beard, Priestess of Dwurfater (Clr5):** HP 22; AC 3[16]; **Atk** *+1 warhammer* (1d4+1); **Move** 9; **Save** 11; **AL** L; **CL/XP** 5/240; **Special:** +2 save vs. paralyzation and poison, +4 save vs. magic, banish undead, darkvision (60ft), spells (2/2).
**Spells:** 1st—*detect evil, protection from evil*; 2nd—*bless, hold person*.
**Equipment:** plate mail armor, *+1 warhammer, potion of levitate*, scroll (*cure light wounds* [x5]), scroll (*cure serious wounds* [x3]).

**Dwarf Guards, Male or Female Dwarves (Ftr3) (11):** HD 3; AC 5[14]; **Atk** polearm (1d8); **Move** 9; **Save** 12; **AL** L; **CL/XP** 3/60; **Special:** +4 save vs. magic, darkvision (60ft), multiple attacks (3) vs. creatures with 1 or fewer HD. (***Monstrosities*** 149)
**Equipment:** chainmail, polearm.
**Kainhis, Hezrou Demon:** HD 9; HP 65; AC –2[21]; **Atk** 2 claws (1d3), bite (4d4); **Move** 6 (fly 12); **Save** 6; **AL** C; **CL/XP** 11/1700; **Special:** immune to fire, magic resistance (50%), spell-like abilities, summon demons (20% chance, hezrou). (***Monstrosities*** 96)
**Spell-like abilities:** at will—*darkness 15ft radius, detect invisibility, fear*.

Kainhis is the leader of the siege. This is a high honor for her to be granted such a command. Her actions past this room through entering the catacombs are described in the timeline above. Orcus is actually using Kainhis as a vanguard. If Kainhis is successful — and without the characters assisting the dwarves, she very well could be — then Orcus' reliance is well-placed. If Kainhis fails, Orcus sends the guards at the *gate* (**Encounter III-E**) to acquire the necessary rune.

# Encounter III-C: Mommy!
## (Area C-2)

The heat in the room is oppressive. Numerous twisting metal pipes run along the walls. Smoke fills the air, and flames roar from large forges. In the center of the room are a number of anvils that form a circle around a small statue of a dwarven deity. The deity has a disapproving look on his face as he glares down on the anvils.

No one works at the forges. The dwarven smiths in long aprons sit cross-legged on the floor in the circle around two plump and cherub-faced dwarven women. The women seem to be telling a story of some sort.

The dwarven women speak in soothing tones as they tells the smiths a fable about a little dwarf lost in the great maze of caverns below the surface world. The characters hear part of the tale as they approach, which ends when the lost dwarf's mother finds the little dwarf and escapes the clutches of an evil elf. At the end, both of the dwarven women ask their audience, "Who wants a kiss from mommy?" Two unlucky dwarves eagerly jump up and are smothered by the women.

Unless they intervene, the characters watch in horror as both smiths drop lifelessly to the floor with gigantic grins on their faces. The dwarven women lick their bloody lips and glare at the characters.

The women are **2 succubi** who have enraptured the group of dwarves. They ask the characters if they are interested in a kiss. At the same time, the succubi command the dwarves to protect their mommies. The dwarves are happy to oblige and aghast that anyone threatens their mothers.

**Dwarf Guards, Male or Female Dwarves (Ftr3) (8):** HD 3; HP 16, 13x2, 12, 11, 9, 3x2; AC 4[15]; **Atk** warhammer (1d4); **Move** 9; **Save** 12; **AL** L; **CL/XP** 3/60; **Special:** +4 save vs. magic, darkvision (60ft), multiple attacks (3) vs. creatures with 1 or fewer HD. (***Monstrosities*** 149)
**Equipment:** chainmail, shield, warhammer.
**Succubus Demon (2):** HD 6; HP 45, 42; AC 9[10]; **Atk** 2 scratches (1d3), kiss (level drain); **Move** 12 (fly 18); **Save** 11; **AL** C; **CL/XP** 9/1100; **Special:** +1 or better magic weapons to hit, level drain (1 level, save resists), magic resistance (70%), spell-like abilities, summon demon (40% chance, baalroch). (***Swords & Wizardry Complete Rulebook*** 97)
**Spell-like abilities:** at will—*charm person, clairaudience, clairvoyance, ESP, polymorph self, suggestion*.
**Tactics:** The succubi attempt to use *suggestion* on the characters to convince them that their weapons and armor are on fire (in an attempt to get them to drop and strip off their weapons). They also try to cast *charm person* on the strongest member of the party. If successful, the succubi try to "kiss" the charmed character. Meanwhile, the enraptured dwarves attack, believing that the party members are demons (due to a *suggestion*).

If the party is accompanying a group of dwarves from one of the previous encounters, these dwarves hesitate to attack their brethren. Instead, they try to flank their brothers to get to the succubi.

Eventually, the "mommies" and the dwarves wander the complex and begin wreaking havoc. As a possible wandering encounter, if the succubi have enraptured a large number of dwarven men, then a group of dwarven women wanting to get their men back might join the characters against the succubi.

# Encounter III-D: The Traitor Kinst and the Devil Spy
## (Area C-3)

This room is a blast of purple, pink, and orange colors. A number of colorful chalk drawings on the room show the Devil's Finger. There is a simple cot with a bright purple blanket. A large wooden dresser of enameled orange is on one side of the room. A large mirror stands on top of the dresser.

The particularly foul Kinst hides here while the demons maraud through the lower level. He talks in hushed tones to the the mirror, but the mirror does not respond. The mirror is a magical scrying device that allowed Kinst to communicate with Orcus and plan the assault. Orcus does not answer Kinst now because he has much better things to do. The mirror functions like a *crystal ball*. The mirror loses all magical properties if removed from the dresser.

## GREATER MISCELLANEOUS MAGICAL ITEM

### TOTEM OF THE GATE

A *totem of the gate* is a magical device that opens a *gate* behind lead or a magical shield. The totem is six inches long and looks like a chalk stick carved in the shape of a demon. To activate the totem, the user draws the appropriate pentagram on a surface. The totem is a one-time use item. The *gate* is thereafter permanent and impervious to any magical attack (i.e., *dispel magic*, and so forth). The only means of eliminating the *gate* is by breaking the totem in half, which destroys the magic and causes all creatures that have traversed the *gate* in either direction to disappear and reappear on their home plane.

Kinst is a coward, a cheat, and thoroughly evil. The High Priest Usis had a soft spot in his heart for Kinst and believed he could be a great priest dedicated to Dwurfater. Because of this love, Usis was blind to his disciple's treacherous nature.

After Usis predicted the demonic invasion, Kinst poisoned him by coating a manuscript with poison. Usis still has stains from this poison on his fingers. A jar containing one dose of the poison called "demon's ink" is hidden in a locked box under Kinst's cot. The poison is an oil-smelling tar. Anyone opening the jar should make a saving throw to avoid initially touching the poison. Anyone failing the save takes 2d6 points of damage.

Kinst used a magical *totem of the gate* that Orcus instructed him to make (see sidebar). Only through Orcus' direct intervention was Kinst able to create the device, which allowed him to open a *gate* in the armory (**Area C-4**). Kinst did so and immediately fled to this room. The totem is on a leather thong around Kinst's neck.

Kinst attempts to deceive the characters and says that he is praying for Usis. He acts as if he is ignorant, but he tries to sneak off if combat becomes a possibility. Kinst may also try to give the characters a spare manuscript poisoned with demon's ink, saying that it is a map of the catacombs or other useful information. The manuscript is in the top drawer of his dresser.

A bone devil lurks here in the Ethereal Plane. The devil was sent to gather information about the key and the vault. Kinst originally tried to bargain with the devil's master, but did not agree to the devil's "commission" for assisting Kinst. The devil instead sent his spy to infiltrate the Citadel.

The bone devil remains hidden in the Ethereal Plane and does not attack unless provoked. Instead, the spy follows them to gain information about their quest. The details of the adventure's outcome depend on whether or not the spy is still alive by the time the characters leave through the lower archway. Note that the size of the Ethereal Plane here is the same as the Citadel's demiplane. Touching the Ethereal Plane here does not allow one to leave the plane and travel anywhere but on the Citadel's demiplane.

**Kinst, Female Dwarf Cabal of the Beard, Priestess of Dwurfater (Clr8):** HP 43; AC 3[16]; Atk *+1 battleaxe* (1d8); **Move** 9; **Save** 6 (+2, ring); **AL** C; **CL/XP** 8/800; **Special:** +2 save vs. paralyzation and poison, +4 save vs. magic, control undead, darkvision (60ft), spells (2/2/2/2/2).
**Spells:** 1st—*cure light wounds* (x2); 2nd—*hold person, silence 15ft radius*; 3rd—*cure disease, speak with dead*; 4th—*cure serious wounds* (x2); 5th—*commune, finger of death*.
**Equipment:** chainmail, tattered white robes, *+1 battleaxe, ring of poison resistance, ring of protection +2, totem of the gate.*
**Bone Devil:** HD 8; HP 55; AC 1[18]; Atk bite (1d6), 2 claws (1d6), bone hook (1d8 + grab), sting (3d4 + poison); **Move** 12; **Save** 8; **CL/XP** 12/2000; **Special:** +1 or better magic weapon to hit, immunities (cold, poison), magic resistance (35%), poison (save or die), resistances (acid, cold) (50%), spell-like abilities. (see **Appendix B: New Monsters**)

## ENCOUNTER II-E: THE GATE (AREA C-5)

This room is the epicenter of the demons' breach. After the *gate* opened here, the demons secured the southern section of the lower level. Currently, the hezrou Kainhis is attempting to force her way into taking Galm and the only *portal rune* that leads to the catacombs.

**Gleegog, Glabrezu Demon:** HD 10; AC –4[23]; Atk 2 pincers (2d6),
2 claws (1d3), bite (1d6); **Move** 9; **Save** 5; **AL** C; **CL/XP** 15/2900; **Special:** immune to fire, magic resistance (60%), spell-like abilities, summon demon (30% chance, roll 1d4 for type: 1–vrock; 2–hezrou; 3–glabrezu; 4–nalfeshnee). (***Monstrosities*** 94)
**Spell-like abilities:** at will—*darkness 15ft radius, fear, levitate, polymorph self.*
**Tarashix, Vrock Demon:** HD 8; HP 60; AC 0[19]; Atk beak (1d6), 2 foreclaws (1d8), 2 rear claws (1d6); **Move** 12 (fly 18); **Save** 8; **AL** C; **CL/XP** 11/1700; **Special:** immune to fire, magic resistance (50%), spell-like abilities, summon demon (10% chance, vrock). (***Monstrosities*** 105)
**Spell-like abilities:** at will—*darkness 15ft radius.*

The characters should attempt to close the *gate*, yet they are under no obligation to do so. If the characters are successful in closing the *gate* by destroying the totem (see **Encounter III-D**), they in effect banish instantaneously every demon who passed through the *gate*. Reinforcements may arrive through the *gate* every 15 rounds. Every 15 rounds, roll 1d12 and consult the table below. Note that additional vrocks and hezrous appear only once. If you roll their associated number again, nothing arrives.

| 1d12 | Reinforcement |
| --- | --- |
| 1–8 | Nothing arrives |
| 9 | **Dretch** |
| 10 | **Succubus** |
| 11 | **Vrock** |
| 12 | **Hezrou** |

**Dretch Demons (1d6+2):** HD 4; AC 2[17]; Atk 2 claws (1d4), bite (1d6); **Move** 9; **Save** 13; **AL** C; **CL/XP** 6/400; **Special:** spell-like abilities. (***Monstrosities*** 92)
**Spell-like abilities:** 1/day—*darkness 15ft radius*, stinking cloud (20ft radius, save or nauseated for 1d4+1 rounds), summon 1d4 giant rats.
**Second-Category Demon (Hezrou Type):** HD 9; AC –2[21]; Atk 2 claws (1d3), bite (4d4); **Move** 6 (fly 12); **Save** 6; **AL** C; **CL/XP** 11/1700; **Special:** immune to fire, magic resistance (50%), spell-like abilities, summon demons (20% chance, hezrou). (***Monstrosities*** 96)
**Spell-like abilities:** at will—*darkness 15ft radius, detect invisibility, fear.*
**Succubus Demon:** HD 6; AC 9[10]; Atk 2 scratches (1d3), kiss (level drain); **Move** 12 (fly 18); **Save** 11; **AL** C; **CL/XP** 9/1100; **Special:** +1 or better magic weapons to hit, level drain (1 level, save resists), magic resistance (70%), spell-like abilities, summon demon (40% chance, baalroch). (***Swords & Wizardry Complete Rulebook*** 97)
**Spell-like abilities:** at will—*charm person, clairaudience, clairvoyance, ESP, polymorph self, suggestion.*
**Vrock Demon:** HD 8; AC 0[19]; Atk beak (1d6), 2 foreclaws (1d8), 2 rear claws (1d6); **Move** 12 (fly 18); **Save** 8; **AL** C; **CL/XP** 11/1700; **Special:** immune to fire, magic resistance (50%), spell-like abilities, summon demon (10% chance, vrock). (***Monstrosities*** 105)
**Spell-like abilities:** at will—*darkness 15ft radius.*

**Tactics:** Gleegog and Tarashix are already bored. Although they had the pleasure of leading the surprise attack into the Citadel, the thrill quickly faded as no real challenge has presented itself. Their current master Orcus whipped the demons into a frenzy when he promised them a river of blood and fresh souls. When they stepped through the portal and saw only a throng of angry dwarves, however, they rolled their eyes and commenced the slaughter. Neither demon can summon any allies due to the magic protecting the Citadel. If Gleegog dies, Tarashix continues to fight, but if the battle seems hopeless, he rushes back through the *gate*. While Tarashix never negotiates, Gleegog is willing to do anything to reach the *gate*.

## CONCLUDING THE CHAPTER

Once the characters convince King Galm of their intentions (likely through saving the day and defeating the demons and exposing Kinst), he is amenable to giving them the *portal rune* to the catacombs. Galm has Usis or another priest inscribe the rune above the one used to enter the Citadel. This rune is of Dwurfater's anvil.

Many dwarves openly disagree with Galm's decision to allow the characters into the catacombs. Although the debate is hostile and open, no dwarves make a move to stop the characters. Ultimately, the division over the decision leads to the downfall of the dwarves.

As the characters step through the portal, they travel once against through time and space and enter the catacombs.